DRONE CHILD

A NOVEL OF WAR, FAMILY, AND SURVIVAL

DAVID H. ROTHMAN

DAVID H. ROTHMAN (ALEXANDRIA, VIRGINIA)

DRONE CHILD: A NOVEL OF WAR, FAMILY, AND SURVIVAL

Revised edition. December 2021

ISBNs:

Paperback: 978-1-7367831-9-1

Hardback: 979-8-9851818-0-7

Kindle: 978-1-7367831-8-4

ePub: 978-1-7367831-7-7

PDF: 979-8-9851818-1-4

Audiobook: 978-1-7367831-6-0

In memory of Carly Rothman, lover of books, Jimmy Dean Sausage Biscuits, and me.

Thanks to the late Ray Arco (for his contributions to the screenplay version).

Also to Junior Boweya and Jean Félix Mwema Ngandu in the Democratic Republic of the Congo. They fact-checked and provided other feedback.

Likewise my thanks to my editor, Dave Pasquantonio, and cover designer, Nate Allison.

Please note that the main story happens not in today's DRC but in the near future. Also keep in mind that this book is far more about relationships than weapons and military strategy.

Appreciate Drone Child? A few heartfelt words on your favorite store or library site will really help—especially if you explain why you liked it. Thanks! - D.R.

TO MY READERS

The problem with a war memoir is there's no suspense. You already know I live.

You also need to know that I not only survive, I thrive. Even less suspense. But such is the nature of the horrors I'll share with you. I doubt you would finish this book without a hint of my happy ending despite all the death and other sadness along the way.

Perhaps my life will inspire you. May it! I'm richer than I ever expected in both love and money. Yes, I was lucky—fate easily could have flattened me. All I could do was *try*.

—Lemba Adula, Kinshasa, Democratic Republic of the Congo, July 18, 2050

CONTENTS

1

———

THE DEATHS OF PAPA AND
MAMA BOULE-BOULE

PEOPLE CALLED ME "THE FIX-IT BOY." I repaired broken radios and TVs around our village of Zange.

Our huts and ramshackle shacks could have used fixing on a grander scale. But I was too busy tinkering, helping my parents, and being 15 years old to care.

I could go on, about my Zange days and my rags-to-riches journey, but I need to start with Mpasi, so you'll know why my sister and I left. Mpasi lied often. But the tremble in his voice and the slight shake in his hands told me there could be only truth in the story he shared months later after we met. Mpasi recalled every detail.

His father was a kind but half-crazy fisherman. People nicknamed Mpasi's parents "Mama and Papa Boule-boule" because most everything they wore had polka dots in it, just like clowns' costumes, even if the dots were smaller. Back then, he must have smiled as often as his parents did.

It all ended the day the rebels shelled Mpasi's riverside village, which, like mine, was about 120 kilometers from Kinshasa, capital of the Democratic Republic of the Congo.

The men drew nearer to collect their bounty. They stole not just food, TVs, and cellphones but also boys and girls to be child soldiers in the war with the central government. Mpasi was 13 at the time, wide-eyed and thin, small for his age. His parents were wearing white clothes with just a touch of polka dots, and the white might have been what killed them—they were all too easy to spot.

A pair of vile rebel officers, dressed in khakis with the insignia of the Congolese Purification Army, closed in on Mama and Papa Boule-boule while they were hiding Mpasi and the two baby boys in the tall bushes just up the road from their village.

I would be unlucky enough to run across these repugnant beasts in time on my own, so I can tell you more about them. "Tiny's" name was a joke. He was really a hulking goateed man with a little bald spot on top. Tiny was middle-aged and the Purification Army's main leader, fond of going out to do his own killing rather than just watch his soldiers at work. Sako was in his 30s, far smaller, with yellow-greenish teeth the color of vomit.

Tiny and Sako yelled at the family to come out of the bushes, which they did, encouraged by the sight of Tiny's AK-47.

"Sako?" Tiny said.

Lieutenant Vomit Tooth pulled out a knife.

"Today," Tiny told Mpasi's father, "your boy becomes a proud member of the Congolese Purification Army." He laughed sardonically and beckoned to Mpasi. "Come here."

Mpasi reluctantly moved forward.

"A good soldier always follows orders," Sako said. "Your first is to kill your parents."

"But," Mpasi said, "I love my parents."

Sako held the knife to Mpasi's neck while Tiny placed the machine gun in the 13-year-old's hands. Tiny made certain Mpasi pointed it at his father and mother.

"Now," Tiny said, "you'll have many parents. These first two are just God's accidents. The Purification Army—we're your new family. God's will!"

Sako pressed the tip of the knife into the boy's flesh, just enough to make him hurt.

"Kill us, Mpasi," begged his mother, still holding the two babies. "Better that they not kill us all."

"Listen to your parents," Sako said in a mock-kindly paternal voice.

Mpasi's father nodded.

Then the boy fired at his parents, who crumpled to the ground, their polka dot clothes stained with blood.

Mpasi, however, had taken pain not to hit the baby brothers his mother had been holding—he aimed for her head.

At the moment, all three brothers were crying.

"Now, now, Mpasi," said Tiny, "where's your compassion? Why are your little brothers still alive? Do you really want to leave them behind for the hyenas to eat?"

Once again, Sako pressed the end of the knife blade into Mpasi's neck. Tiny forced Mpasi to point the gun at the younger brothers, still clinging to the parents' corpses.

"Do it," Sako said, "and soon you'll eat cake and watch movies with the other boys."

Sako's knife went a tad deeper to encourage Mpasi to get on with the killing. But then Tiny grabbed the gun away from the boy.

"We are not cruel men," Tiny said. "I'll kill the babies myself."

Then he pulled the trigger.

And so all the others died while Mpasi lived.

How could that *not* have changed him in time? I would like to think he was born without the slightest touch of evil. But sometimes it happens accidentally, like a boulder rolling down a hill to crush you when you're just walking by.

2

—————

THE BURNING OF OUR
PALACE OF DREAMS

I HADN'T YET MET Mpasi, but his family's fate was exactly what I feared for my parents, sister, and me. Family first—especially when soldiers kill, rape, and pillage!

This being my war memoir, I'll write of AK-47s, machetes, drones, blood, and charred bodies. But please refrain from dismissing the people of the Democratic Republic of the Congo as simply murderers and victims. Killing each other—is that all you think we've done, other than die of Ebola? We also are a country of dreamers, artists, musicians, and other creators, and you can start with my precious family.

Michel Adula, father of me, Lemba, was a farmer-fisherman somewhat like Mpasi's papa. He was also an orphan married to another, Heloise, who helped him grow bananas and other food. The orphanage that raised them was but a vague memory in time, its records lost just like so much of our country's past.

The orphanage staffers had not shared the slightest hint of my parents' origins, or other children's, lest this distract the wards from connections with *them*. Institutional ties above all, in deference to the bizarre theories of a racist Belgian childcare professor! "The children's pasts," he had pontificated in a jargon-infested tome which certain orphanages used as a bible, "must never be permitted to distract professionals from their goal of human perfectibility." Years later I would read how this man's work had been subsidized by our country's colonizers to help rationalize the destruction of Congolese families and the promotion of child labor. Children—another resource to be exploited as avidly as timber and diamonds!

Both my parents were short, with narrow faces and soft voices, the kind of people bullies love to push around. Meek and obscure, intelligent but no geniuses, they seemed destined to be that way forever. But my parents still urged my twin sister and me to dream, and I'd like to think we *all* succeeded. The very language of this book suggests that I have reached a certain level of schooling far beyond Mama and Papa's. I'd hope that my French—the original or in translation—would not disappoint you.

In birth and spirit, Josiane and I were still our parents' children, but to their delight, the Almighty somehow had willed that we be different. We were bully-proof, both tall for our age, with athletic bodies as well as sharp minds.

By the time we were 15—that's when my memoir really begins—Josiane was already drawing stares from some older men. I am uncomfortable writing of this, especially when she was so young. But her shape and her voice helped make her who she was or might be. Josiane dreamed of becoming a professional singer of Congolese rumba, the sweet dance music you heard everywhere. She spent hours watching music videos on our ancient color television.

YouTube music was a different matter, a rarity at first in

Josiane's life. We were too poor then for the Internet and cellphones or a satellite dish to pirate TV programs.

Except on cellphones, the Net had yet to reach our village. I would borrow a phone from any friend who owned one. At first, I could just mooch a few minutes here and there. But I had such a knack for technology that before long, my friends were *pleading* for me to accept their loans.

After all, I could help them figure out this glitch, that software app, or the secret of moving to the next level in a game. I couldn't get enough—I'd found my niche and even could earn some stray Congolese francs to augment my Fix-It Boy money.

I imagined the software apps as animals, each with its own terrain and set of habits. Mastering the software was like hunting. I would make mistakes, analyze my failures, and in time puzzle out the patterns to succeed again and again. In ordinary life, that was exactly how I learned to trap and shoot bushmeat for myself and my family—not for sport, not for killing's sake, but rather to help survive lean times. By nature, my gentle parents themselves were more farmers at heart than hunters.

Not every village in the Congo is or was like ours in its ambitions for its sons and daughters, but the condition of the one-room wooden schoolhouse hinted of something. It was the best-built, best-maintained building in Zange, as if the villagers were trying to tell the teacher to care as much about the children's minds.

I would soon see the cruel handiwork of Tiny and Sako, the thugs from the Congolese Purification Army, after they rudely interrupted my school day. Thank God I didn't meet them face to face when they and their Purifiers raided—such horrors would come later.

Monsieur Songa, the buck-toothed village teacher, had been lecturing us that day on the great inventors of the world, or at least doing a reasonable job of parroting from the textbooks.

Thunderstorms had raged earlier in the week, but now it was sunny and clear—too halcyon a day for anything to go wrong. I was wearing tattered shorts, and Josiane was in a simple cotton-print dress, both of us ready for some goof-off time with friends after school. The boys would kick around a football while the girls watched.

"And who," asked Monsieur Songa, "was the American Thomas Edison, and what did he invent?" Oh, please, Monsieur! A little more of a challenge! Bored or not, however, Josiane and I raised our hands. No one else did.

Monsieur Songa shook his head. "No, no, give the others a chance." Silence. "Okay," he said, "Lemba?"

"The first practical light bulb," I said. "Not everyone agreed on that, but—"

Suddenly a loud bell rang from the village's center, and Père Kasongo, our priest and the village leader, burst into the schoolhouse. "The Purifiers are coming! Run home and tell your parents." A man in a village nearby had phoned in the warning.

Père Kasongo told us to get our families and go a mile up the road to a hiding place marked by a pile of rocks—no time for packing even a few belongings.

"Class dismissed!" Monsieur Songa said as if *he* were the one who most counted, and the students scurried out the schoolhouse door.

AND SO, not knowing whether we'd have homes to return to, most everyone in and near the village fled to the designated area, muttering curses at the Kinshasa government for failing to protect us.

No small number of Zange's adults speculated as to which politicians and military officers might have been bribed to allow the Congolese Purification Army to roam free. Even there in the high bushes, with our voices kept low, we feared that the thugs would find and murder us.

The government radio station said the Purification Army members loved to experiment with different tools for killing. Typically, the "Purifiers" used a mix of AK-47s, other guns, rocket-propelled grenades, and machetes, for they took special pleasure in dismembering victims and mounting their heads on posts. Again and again, the Purifiers would litter the ground with stray legs and arms. Government clean-up crews did not visit every village post-massacre, but when they did, they often wore gloves to guard against germs from the carnage.

Hiding from the Purifiers, my parents and sister and I snacked on dried fruit chips. Our dog Kodjo, a pure-bred Congolese Terrier with pointed ears and nose and short black-and-white hair, wasn't with us. The sounds of his movements through the bush might otherwise give our location away.

Papa had won Kodjo in a raffle. To be precise, Kodjo was a Basenji, or "dog of the bush." That meant he couldn't bark, just grunt and growl, but he was the perfect hunting dog and the terror of the local river rats. We figured Kodjo would be smart enough to reunite with us eventually without the Purifiers having discovered whose dog he was. I hoped he'd keep his distance from them anyway, but to be safe, we removed the bells that normally tinkled on him.

Mama put her arms around Josiane to comfort her and softly prayed that somehow the Purifiers would change their sick minds at the last minute and destroy another village instead. But when we looked in the direction of Zange, smoke was spiraling up into the sky.

Like the others, we waited a day before returning. Josiane and I wandered around the village calling out for Kodjo. No luck. Perhaps we shouldn't have let him loose. The Purifiers just might be sadistic enough to kill him on sight. Of course, they might also have stolen him to be a pet. He was that endearing, with his handsome long-snouted face and soft fur. But no! I just couldn't imagine the Purifiers owning pets.

We wept over the blackened remains of the wooden schoolhouse, the source of the smoke. Of course! The Purifiers had attacked our little palace of dreams. They had also urinated in our church. Thoroughly loathsome people. Certain houses were missing TVs, radios, jewelry, and other valuables as well as food, but the Purification Army had set afire just the schoolhouse. A note taped to the bell in the center of the village explained why:

"Next time we burn everything and look harder for you. Tell the government we will protect you now. This visit, just a warning—only the school."

THE PURIFIERS HADN'T STOLEN a thing from us, big surprise. Who would bother? We lived in a small two-room wooden shack with a saggy old couch, mattresses on the floor, a scratched-up dining table, a tin roof, and on-again-off-again electric service from a generator for the neighborhood. No refrigerator. Just a wood-burning stove attached to a chimney. A TV antenna for local reception topped a ten-meter pipe in the backyard.

Mama flicked on our small-screened television, which struggled to pull in staticky signals from a government station halfway between us and the capital.

The Purifier story led the news, with mention of carnage from the nearby village of Sambuka: "New horrors, some 120 kilometers south of Kinshasa." Later, I'd meet Mpasi and learn this was the same massacre where his parents and brothers had died seven kilometers up-river from me.

As usual, the government reminded us of the Purifiers kidnapping children and forcing them to kill their parents. The rebels' goal was for the young ones not to have any families to return to. A little like the orphanage staffers wiping out my parents' past to instill greater attachment to the institution. The Purifiers could turn even seven- or eight-year-olds into obedient killers. The smallest child soldiers so often were the best—less able to tell right from wrong or safe from dangerous, smaller targets for enemies, and in need of less food to fuel their killing. They didn't even demand salaries. If only the Purifiers had limited themselves to the younger children—bad enough by itself! But they were also in search of teenagers for both military purposes and the provision of "wives" for the troops.

Mama cranked down the volume. We'd heard enough. Kodjo, who'd returned the previous day, flopped on his back as if in search of another belly rub. I obliged him while we talked on.

"Where have these people been?" Papa said of the government news reader's repetition of the obvious. "On the moon?"

"I'd never kill you," I said. "I'd die first."

"Me, too," said Josiane.

"They're coming back," Mama said. "I just know it."

THE VILLAGE ELDERS would have loved to pay off the Central Government's Army enough to do its job and keep the killers away. But that was for much richer people. So Purifiers could roam free and terrorize us, especially since they were among the most dependable bribers.

All we could do was pray and distract ourselves with the rebuilding of the schoolhouse.

Every able-bodied adult and child above a certain age sawed and hammered away. Within a month a new building arose, complete with murals painted on the walls.

Did I not say we are, in part, a nation of artists and other creative people? My sister's dancing and singing, of course, won the talent competition held to celebrate the completion of the new schoolhouse. All eyes were on Josiane as she belted out an old classic from Mbilia Bel, "La Cléopatre de la Musique Congolaise."

"Enjoy Josiane while you can, before she leaves us for Kinshasa," said Père Kasongo, the village leader.

"Or Hollywood," joked Monsieur Songa, the schoolteacher.

"No, Paris," said Père Kasongo, and turned to my sister. "Josiane—where to?"

"How about both?" Josiane teemed with self-confidence, and to everyone in the village, that just made her all the more attractive.

The others might never escape the mud and the dust and the threats from terrorists, but through Josiane, maybe they could live out their dreams.

A MONTH later the Purifiers burned, raped, and pillaged their way through more of the neighboring villages. Scores more parents died at the hands of their own children.

Père Kasongo feared he would once again have to ring his bell.

Our society was sick, and amid a drought, our vegetable gardens and orchards didn't fare much better. As my parents worked at harvesting the pathetic crop of oranges, Josiane and I went fishing in our little river to help take care of our food needs of the moment.

"Maybe," she said, adjusting her net, "it's time to leave Zange. Too many nightmares. Do you dream what I dream? Of Mama and Papa. Of having to kill them. So far God has spared us. But for how long?"

As never before, the Purifiers were kidnapping children and forcing them to do the unthinkable. How many more months or years would this go on? Did the Purifiers have a patricide and matricide quota? Even older children, normally just slaughtered without further ado, became forced murderers.

"But who says it will happen to us?" I asked.

"The longer we stay," Josiane said, "the more likely. It's time to go."

"But you haven't finished your schooling."

"What schooling?" she said. "All Monsieur Songa does is repeat his books." And guess which two students had already borrowed and read most of the books from his small library? He was a good teacher in the eyes of the parents of Zange. It's just that Monsieur Songa hadn't that much to teach *us*.

"I'll miss you," I said.

"No, you won't," Josiane said. "Because you're coming with me."

"To Kinshasa?"

"You could always find a job fixing gadgets."

I nodded. Surely enough televisions and radios were on the blink in a city of millions for me to find work at a repair shop before I opened up my own. I had a vague idea of inventing things, too. A new kind of TV? A cellphone? Thomas Edison hadn't gone to college. Must I? My 15-year-old self didn't dream of riches or a university education, just a chance to tinker with wires and printed circuit boards and software coding for video games. I could hunt and fish as well as the next village child, but gadgets excited *me*.

Of the two of us, Josiane at the time was the more ambitious. But then again, what's ambition? In Zange, it seemed remarkable enough just to end up running a TV repair shop in Kinshasa. Forget the inventions. They could come later.

In other ways, Josiane and I were so alike. It's said you can separate certain twins and they will grow up with similar tastes in music and art and most everything else in life without the least contact between them. Same for physical mannerisms. Not all twins are that way, but Josiane and I shared a gene-deep twin connection where we could almost communicate without a word spoken. Our blood bond made us care all the more about each other. We even had bluish triangle-shaped birthmarks in the same place near our left ankles—further affirmation of the Almighty's vision for us.

Told of our plans at dinner that evening, my parents were skeptical at first; didn't they need us in the fields?

"Please," I said, "the best way to love you is to leave you. No kids around, you stay alive." In the worlds of both nightmares and reality, it was as simple as that.

"Two fewer mouths to feed," said Josiane.

"And lots of places in Kinshasa," I said, "for her to sing." But to tell the truth, the Purifier-related fears mattered just as much as our respective ambitions.

We all wept at the bus stop. "Here," Mama said, handing us a small pouch of money for the road. "Not much, but a little more will help."

Josiane shook her head. "You need this for yourself. Lemba and I will find work immediately."

"No, take it."

My sister and I hesitated a second, then accepted the money just as the old diesel bus was pulling up. And then Josiane gave the pouch back.

I rubbed Kodjo's belly one last time and wished I could say good-bye and tell him why I was leaving. Though he was a family dog, I liked to think he was more mine than everyone else's. Of course, all the other Adulas felt the same way.

Still teary-eyed, Josiane and I reached out to Mama and Papa for our final hugs.

3

THE TRADE OF SURVIVING

It was our first trip to Kinshasa. What we saw, in the outer parts, did not in the least resemble the glass-and-steel skyscrapers and posh restaurants that the government propaganda channel touted.

Through the rolled-down windows—no air conditioning on this bus—we saw rickety shacks with rusty roofs, colorful but ragged clothes hanging out to dry, semi-naked children playing in the streets, and ruffians shaking fists at each other.

"Awful," I told Josiane. "I thought life would be *better* here."

"Oh, come on," said Josiane, "it can't all be like this."

In fact, as we reached the center of town, we did see some high-rises as well as wide boulevards and green patches of park. At first glance this could have been America or Europe with palm trees, except we'd never visited either place.

"Told you," Josiane exulted. "Aren't you glad we came?"

I won't waste time telling you of all the possible

employers who turned us down the first day. *A job, please—now!* Josiane and I had saved some cash on our own, but we should have accepted Mama's money pouch. Josiane could not find a gig as a singer, and I flopped at getting hired as a fix-it-guy. Nor could an ill-dressed teenager from the bush obtain a job at one of the staid "digital spaces" for tech entrepreneurs who wanted a faster Internet, conference rooms, and a chance to goof off from time to time on video games.

The nearest we came to work was at Pierre's Internet Café, which I later discovered was among the last still left in Kinshasa. Through the grimy windows, a large computer monitor displayed a video game, and the dazzle drew us inside, where we heard loud beeps emanating from a speaker. Perhaps a place for the two of us? Josiane could sing and I could help people with the Internet and other geekish matters.

Rumba music played in the background. Few customers were around, but the room still reeked of leftover cigarette smoke. The carpet was decorated with a series of crazy multi-color swirls, much like the walls.

Pierre's was dimly lit, illuminated mainly by the light from a row of flat-screen computer monitors in front. Worn-out plastic tables surrounded a performing area farther inside the room. If this was modern Kinshasa, maybe we needed to refine our pickpocketry and save up for a flight to Paris.

We asked for Pierre's owner-manager. He was a balding man in his fifties with a bloated face suggesting too much booze, and he frowned on seeing us. We both were wearing shabby, baggy clothes—Josiane's exact shape was invisible.

"Leave," he said. "No riffraff."

"Please," I said, "I know the best games to download. A chance, Monsieur." Josiane and I both made our case. I told how I could unfreeze balky apps and coach customers. The Fix-It Boy in new surroundings! "Well," said the owner, whose full name we learned was Pierre Zumbu, "maybe if you buy some better clothes."

We slept that night under an overpass with the traffic rumbling overhead. Or tried to. A fat policeman roused us. "You there," he said, "that'll be 1,000 francs."

"But we have only 4,000," I said.

"We need everything for food," Josiane said.

"Then," the policeman said, "you can no longer stay here." He threw up his hands as if he could do nothing. "There are laws, and there are fees."

"For sleeping under a bridge?" I asked.

The policeman laughed. "You must be new in town. Here we do things differently. You need to meet Doka."

"Who is Doka?"

"Sleep here for just 500 francs tonight. Tomorrow I'll take you to him."

Doka turned out to be a gimlet-eyed man in his late twenties. His flashy clothing made him look like a pimp, which he might have doubled as.

"Nothing to worry about," the policeman said in introducing us. "Doka will take good care of you."

"Would you like breakfast?" Doka said in his shack off one of the main boulevards after the cop left. "We've got fried bananas and rice and fufu and maboke." He pointed to a table with the food, and Josiane and I wolfed it down.

"Rest now," Doka said. "You'll learn the trade in no time."

"What trade?" I asked.

"The trade of surviving."

A DAY later Josiane accosted a wealthy-looking foreign businessman while holding up a fake Rolex. I was behind him, out of his immediate sight.

"Monsieur!" she said. "This is a wonderful watch, but I must sell it."

"Not interested," the businessman said in German-accented French, and kept on walking.

"Oh, but you must buy it. My father is dying of cancer. The operation will cost—"

"I told you," our victim said irritably.

Now I was drawing closer to reach into the man's pocket.

"I'll give it away," Josiane said. "Just 80,000 francs. Less than 50 euros."

"I don't care what the exchange rate is."

A score! I liberated a cellphone from the foreigner.

"God bless you anyway, Monsieur," Josiane said. "*À bientöt.*"

The businessman silently walked off, unaware that his phone had traveled in a different direction. I triumphantly held up the new trophy.

I was ashamed, too, of course, not just proud. Our parents hadn't raised us to be thieves. But this was not Zange—rather, Kinshasa, where they charged for sleeping under overpasses. We were good kids, Josiane and me. But we were also fast learners.

WHEN WE KNOCKED on Pierre Zumbu's office door the next week, I was wearing a new striped shirt and cotton pants, almost on the verge of dressiness. Josiane wore a print dress hugging her curves.

"Ah," he said, "at least a better class of riffraff."

"So we're hired?" I asked.

"*Maybe*," Monsieur Zumbu said. Pause. "All right. I'll give you a try."

I would go on to amaze Monsieur Zumbu's regulars with my natural prowess with the joystick. They gasped as I killed off a giant space alien on the screen far faster than anyone else in the room could. All those hours of hunting for food had not exactly harmed my hand-eye coordination. The joystick was just a distant cousin of my third-hand rifle.

"How do you do it?" a customer asked.

"Takes one to handle one," I said. "I *am* an alien."

"I thought you never played this game before," he said.

"Perhaps in another life."

I shot down yet another UFO attacking the Eiffel Tower.

"Or another planet?" the customer asked.

All this time, Monsieur Zumbu was endlessly more interested in Josiane than in the aliens or the recorded rumba music.

"Nice dress," he said. "You fill it well." He gave a smile as wide as the Congo River.

"Monsieur! I'm a third your age." Her tone suggested polite indignation rather than coquettishness.

"Your brother's a lucky fellow—such a pretty sister."

"Now," said Josiane, "what if you didn't just have recorded music? What if you also had me singing to it? And dancing, too? Do you have a microphone?"

Monsieur Zumbu nodded.

"But what if you drive the customers away?"

"Anything bongo and guitar," Josiane said, "I know all

the hits. Good singing, then lots of drinking. Your customers will spend more."

"OK, let's see what you can do."

Monsieur Zumbu went off to get the microphone, then plugged it into a boombox.

"Listen up!" he shouted over the boombox to the customers. "Josiane here is going to sing for us."

Curious, the games players and Internet surfers stopped and turned around.

"Drinks on the house," Monsieur Zumbu said, "if she's as good as she says. Everyone, tell me what you think!"

He turned on the bongo and guitar music.

"A favorite!" Josiane said. She grabbed the microphone and started dancing while belting out the lyrics. The customers, mostly semi-well-dressed men, couldn't take their eyes off her. They smiled, got up, and danced, swaying along with Josiane. Then the music ended, and the applause began. Some customers even threw money at Josiane, who eagerly picked up the cash.

Monsieur Zumbu stuck his thumb up in approval. "Drinks on the house!"

"*Merci, merci!*" Josiane said.

"Would your parents mind?" Monsieur Zumbu asked. I wondered if he was softening up Josiane for harassment later on. But perhaps not. The flirting and the rest might simply be part of show business. The policeman perhaps had made me too cynical. Josiane and I could work regularly now, and I was happy for both of us.

"We're orphans, Monsieur," she said with a big wink. "30,000 francs a night and no questions."

I just hoped Josiane knew what she might be getting into. But put it this way. Although we'd grown up in a village with few streets, we were still, instinctively, street-smart.

"You heard my sister," I told Monsieur Zumbu. "30,000, or she sings for another café." A large man, wearing a pointed beard and a loud orange shirt hanging outside his purple pants, spoke up.

"Hire her!" he ordered Monsieur Zumbu. "A bargain."

"All right," the café owner said. "30,000."

Josiane and I hugged. How far we'd come since the night spent under the overpass!

4

THE INTERNET CAFÉ

Josiane resisted Monsieur Zumbu's pleas to perform in a bikini-skimpy costume—she would go only so far. It didn't matter. More modestly dressed or not, she could still draw crowds to the point where people were lining up outside the Internet Café just to see her. She had a smooth, confident, heartfelt style and with practice mastered the guitar. Best of all, the results were danceable. How can a country with such ugly wars be home to such beautiful music?

I wasn't doing too badly myself. I attracted my own crowds, and I even did double-duty as a substitute DJ and creator of scam letters to gullible foreigners. I had mixed feelings about the letters. But remember, Kinshasa for me was where the police charged people to sleep under overpasses. I did not consider myself a criminal. I simply worried that the good times would end, and I wanted to save up. Josiane and I also had rent to pay on the little apartment we shared amid the glitter of downtown Kinshasa.

Around then, I even bought myself a little e-scooter to zip around in, and I gained a friend in Junior Boweya, owner of Brainy E-Scooters, who encouraged his customers to hack their machines. My new blind-spot detector helped me survive crazy drivers as I weaved through the streets of Kinshasa. If only I could have invented such a detector to guard against life's other hidden threats!

"Just so you know," Monsieur Zumbu announced one night over the new public address system, "Lemba is offering free Internet lessons tonight. Yes, free. Tonight only!" A crowd eagerly clustered around me. I was becoming more like my sister and learning to enjoy the extra attention.

Along the way, Monsieur Zumbu trained me as an occasional substitute bartender. I learned how to ply customers at the bar with salty nuts so they'd gulp down more martinis. The glasses all had thick bottoms and matte surfaces to make the customers think they were getting more booze than they were.

I also educated myself with Googled articles and YouTube videos. I could learn English and Webmastering, watch a documentary on eighteenth-century pirates, and along the way enjoy old videos starring Petit-Pays, an amazing musician from Cameroon.

Some people need to be there in person to learn. But I could soak up encyclopedia-sized helpings of knowledge from afar. I was and am patient with people lacking such talents. The smartest, most practical learners can get the most out of their knowledge by sharing it with others, whether or not they can immediately return the favor.

I even, just for the fun of it, used YouTube to help master karate and jiu-jitsu and spent hours practicing with an oversized waiter who doubled as our café's bouncer. Call me a peaceful realist. That's the way you had to be on the streets of Kinshasa in case you ended up in the wrong alley.

"Nice work on those letters," Monsieur Zumbu said just

before I stepped out into another dark, dangerous night. "You're a natural scammer. All the others—they just work from scripts."

"Stupid rich people," I said, "are God's gifts." I'd in fact thought about it in more depth. You really had to be a greedster yourself to fall for the scams. I'd never write scam letters today, but back then, before I'd even heard of Robin Hood and the Sheriff of Nottingham, I had my Robin side.

"How'd you like to go with me to the carnival tomorrow?" Monsieur Zumbu asked. "No sister. Just us men." So I went and watched him fire his laser gun futilely at some moving lions on the little target range to the right of the Crocodile Lady, as they called one of the scaly exhibits. "Your turn," he said. I, of course, killed off every lion within sight. A joystick wasn't the only thing I was good at. Nor did my hand-eye coordination fail me when Monsieur Zumbu took me to a real range to shoot clay pigeons.

Peaceful though I considered myself, I enjoyed killing both on screen and at the rifle range. You should have seen me play a US drone operator in a computer game set in the Middle East. I blew up 20 terrorists but not a single civilian. The customers applauded. If the Americans had to kill, I just hoped it worked out that way in real life.

In reality I wouldn't have been eager to kill even *terrorists* with drones if they weren't a direct threat to me. I simply enjoyed the challenge of the game.

WHEN MY SISTER and I bought a big-screen TV, Josiane said, "I know who else would like one." She and I took it along with us on our overdue visit back to Zange. Until now we'd been vague with our parents about our good fortune. What if our sudden luck failed us? Suppose Monsieur Zumbu's café fell out of fashion and the customers stopped coming? Or what if the terrorists struck, as they were wont to at random all over Kinshasa? But so far, so good. It was finally time to share our joy with Mama and Papa in person. At least a slim chance existed that the Purifiers would swoop in and kidnap us while we were back in Zange, but they could have done that to any of the other village children instead. This gamble was worth taking.

My parents were flabbergasted that we could afford an expensive gift, and we realized that the time had come to let them know how far removed we were now from our hand-to-mouth lives on the street. After we set up the TV, Mama and Papa were so caught up in a game show that we had trouble getting their attention. Of course, their fixation on the gift made us all the happier we'd bought it.

"And now," I said finally, "here's our real surprise. Josiane is no longer a waitress, and I—"

"No job," Papa said, "you need to return the television." Children first, regardless of how much he and Mama enjoyed the TV!

Josiane laughed. "Papa! I'm a singer now. Finally."

"How much?"

"Well, people line up to see me. And Lemba also."

"He sings, too?"

"Not quite," I said, "but I am the best Internet guy in town. You want to know something, you come to me. Not bad at video games, either."

"I can't believe it," Josiane said. "People *pay* to have Lemba tutor them."

"All this behind our backs," Mama marveled.

"Actually, my friends here paid me for games tips," I said. "I'm just getting more in Kin."

"We're not done yet," Josiane said, and reached for a small package. Inside was a high-powered cellphone that could reliably work with far-off towers. "No more letters. Now you can hear our voices."

"So many good things happening at once," Mama said. "I hope that doesn't mean bad times ahead."

"Please, Mama," Josiane said, "haven't we been through enough of them already?"

5

"OUR BIGGEST MONEY-MAKER"

Monsieur Zumbu, except for occasionally groping Josiane, was a model boss. The lines of customers grew longer and the pay grew higher, for both of us. To think we had been mere street kids just a few months before! What a kind, generous man, if you could somehow look beyond his loathsome depravity!

Oh, yes, beyond being a letch, he drank heavily and had his oddities such as a goofy smile, and he could be insufferably oily toward anyone whose favor he wanted. And why was he so secretive about the door at the back of the café, the one he always kept locked?

"You are not to follow me," he reprimanded Josiane when she caught him unlocking it with a big, bronze key. But who cared what Monsieur Zumbu did in private? His cash was as good as the cleanest-living churchgoer's. Monsieur Zumbu would allow me plenty of breaks in slow periods, during which I continued my self-education on YouTube.

One day I saw a commercial online for Kids 'N Gadgets

hawking quadcopter drones for the young. That ballyhoo in time would change my life.

The commercial enthralled me. It opened with peppy music, and then a drone hovered above its young owner as he palled around with three nubile girls at a swimming pool. "Your QuadKid Drone," the announcer promised, "will make you the talk of the neighborhood." Then the lucky drone owner watched the video of that pool scene from his living room couch, his arm wrapped around one of the girls' shoulders. Her poolside friends sat on the floor, looking as enthralled as I was. "$28.95 US dollars in most locations," the announcer said. "Available worldwide." I had to get one! Why hadn't I been into the drone scene already? I could discover drones *and* women at the same time. As much as I cared in a respectable family way for Josiane, what was I doing still living with my sister?

Sure enough, Nzazi's TV & Electronics Store in Kinshasa stocked QuadKid Drones. It was dark when I returned to our apartment, and I didn't want to risk myself and the drone amid the traffic outside. So the maiden voyage was inside the living room, where my QuadKid barely missed knocking over a 5,000-franc lamp that Josiane had just bought.

I was tempted to phone in sick to spend more time with the drone. But then I had an idea. Why not make the drone part of my routine at Pierre's Internet Café? Perhaps at some point I could even give drone lessons. So the next night I showed up at Pierre's with the drone and the joystick-style controller. Two customers kept staring at me and the QuadKid—one was the big goateed fellow I'd seen earlier with the orange shirt and purple pants, except that this time he had brought a friend, a smaller man with the rottenest-looking teeth I'd ever seen.

Monsieur Zumbu couldn't stop bragging to them about me. "When we're out hunting...great hearing...sharp eyes...sharp everything...perfect shot!"

"Nice," said the dental nightmare.

"And to think," said Monsieur Zumbu, "a computer genius, too. No one knows the Internet better."

The hulking goateed man pointed a finger at the drone. "Can we fly it inside?"

Monsieur Zumbu grinned. "Lemba, show them."

I deftly maneuvered the QuadKid around the Internet Café and let it hover near the two customers.

"Thank you, Lemba," Monsieur Zumbu said. "I think the gentlemen have seen enough."

"But wait," I said.

I did a few mouse clicks and keystrokes. An "aerial" photo of the two customers appeared on a flat-screen computer monitor nearby.

"Look," the dental nightmare said to his overgrown friend, "it even shows your bald spot."

"We could use a young man like that," said the goateed man who'd worn the orange shirt. "We'd like to know him a *lot* better."

"If you want to learn computer games," I said, "I'll teach you all you need to know. The Internet, too. And if you have a problem with your router, I'm your guy. Pay me enough, I'll even make home visits."

"Listen," said the dental nightmare, "we'd like you to join our business."

"I'm afraid he's quite happy here," Monsieur Zumbu said.

I nodded. "You need to understand. Monsieur Zumbu took my sister and me off the street."

"What if we could buy you a Little Airplane five times that size?" the dental nightmare asked.

I shook my head. "I'm sorry, Monsieur."

The goateed man edged closer to Monsieur Zumbu to emphasize the difference in the men's bulk. "I promise, this is God's will! The boy could have a real future with us."

"But he's our biggest money-maker," Monsieur Zumbu said.

"Exactly why we want him. Smart boy."

"But I still don't even know what you do," my boss said.

"Here's what we do." Without the slightest effort, the big goateed man lifted Monsieur Zumbu high by the armpits.

"So you're debt collectors?"

"For God and the people of the Congo."

He dropped Monsieur Zumbu.

"Next time," said the dental nightmare, "we'll be rougher."

"Yeah," said the goateed man, "we'll be back."

FOR REASONS OF SELF-PRESERVATION, Monsieur Zumbu and I treated our visitors gingerly. But after they left, he pooh-poohed the threat.

Kinshasa was full of crazies. A practitioner of witchcraft had even promised to cast a spell on the Internet Café and make it sink slowly into a bottomless pit if Monsieur Zumbu did not dress his dancers in full-length black robes and veils. But the café didn't descend an inch. Monsieur Zumbu assured me that the goateed bully and his friend had also been bluffing. They had been drinking, and the booze must have been speaking.

One rainy night, Monsieur Zumbu showed up with

bruises on his face and his speech slurred, as if he'd suffered at least a mild concussion. "Clumsy me," he said, and told how he had slipped on the sidewalk. Perhaps out of convenience, I dismissed some dark thoughts about the origins of the concussion.

"Have you been to a hospital?" I asked.

"Nothing to worry about."

"Monsieur, you really should go."

"I know where I want to go. Football game next weekend. Want to come?"

We motorcycled there—I rode at the rear—only to find that Monsieur Zumbu had lost the tickets. "No problem," he said. "I've got friends. Just stay here so our bike doesn't get swiped." And so I did, spending the time talking on the phone with Josiane, who had just called to say she would be on a major TV channel the next week.

"I knew this would happen," I said. "How proud you'll make us all!"

"7 o'clock next Tuesday on Channel Four."

"But aren't you supposed to be working then? What would Monsieur Zumbu say?"

"That he's grateful for the publicity and you can come. Later, dear brother."

As I was hanging up, a black van stopped near me. The goateed man and the dental nightmare approached me, tore my phone away, and dragged me inside the van. It happened lickety-split. I didn't even have enough chance to put up a struggle.

"Please, Monsieurs," I said, "I beg of you—let me go."

The goateed man held me while the dental nightmare went to work with what must have been chloroform, and that was the last I remembered before blacking out.

Revived with smelling salt, I woke up in a tent in the middle of a mix of jungle and bush. Might I be in some kind of military camp? Peering through an opening in the fabric, I could see other tents like this one and even some wooden huts. The dental disaster was by my side, just adding to the terror.

"Where am I?"

"In God's hands now," the dental disaster said.

"Does this mean God is a Purifier?"

Yes, who else could it be? Imagine—I'd fled to Kinshasa, only to fall into the hands of the people whose cruelty I was trying to escape. I couldn't help but think of my parents. Would the Purifiers want me to kill Mama and Papa? I was in a whole different world, a meaner, less hopeful one than the kind I'd been snatched from. I could imagine Josiane's dismay when she eagerly called me about her TV performance and the phone just rang and rang. Oh for her to have scored big with the host and the viewers!

The dental disaster paused for effect and shook his head.

"So," I asked, "you are not the Purification Army?"

"Of course we are. We're not God. Just His friends." Lieutenant Sako Tota, the dental disaster, reintroduced himself. He let me know how blessed I was to encounter him and Tiny, the goateed leader of the Purifiers, while they were taking time out in Kinshasa from their holy killing.

Through the tent opening now, I could see Purifier officers drilling kids in uniform. "You said you were businessmen," I said.

"Oh, but we are," Sako said. "We just use AK-47s to get our fair share in our transactions."

"Take me back to Kinshasa."

"And be a deserter?" Sako said. "You are now in the Congolese Purification Army. Stand proud and cheer for the Purifiers."

A pimply-faced soldier, not much older than I was, handed me a camouflage-patterned uniform.

"Don't even think of escaping," Sako said, "or we'll purify you for sure."

"What does that mean?"

"Kill you."

Sako and the other soldier left. I removed my civilian clothes and changed into the uniform. Then I reached back into my old pants for a picture of me with my parents and sister and stashed it into one of the uniform's pockets. I wondered when or if I would ever see them again. As if Mama and Papa lacked enough things to worry about already—from their crops to the possibility of the Purifiers returning to burn down every hut in the village!

THE NEXT DAY the pimply-faced soldier led me to a drill area, where a number of newly uniformed boys and girls milled around in disarray. Sako was speaking from a wooden platform: "Welcome to the CPA, the Congolese Purification Army. Think of us as God's agents, reclaiming everything stolen by the thieves of Kinshasa! Minerals! Money! Our *dignity*! Everyone, say it: 'Yes, Mon Lieutenant!'"

"Yes, Mon Lieutenant!" we captives repeated.

"No foreign bribes for us!" Sako said. "Just an eternity in heaven. Say it! 'I want to get into heaven, eat cake, and watch movies all day long!'"

"I want to get into heaven, eat cake, and watch movies all day long!" we echoed.

No, I *didn't*. I just wanted to be back in Kinshasa with Josiane, enjoying her wit, warmth, and singing and her unwavering encouragement of my own talents as a techie and substitute DJ. I still associated "now" with the Internet Café—I just couldn't imagine staying in the camp. Of course, the Purifiers had other plans for me.

"And all the girls here," Sako went on, "will bear angel sons who become football stars!" Pause. "But you must obey me. Otherwise your gun will send you to hell."

In another part of the camp, we filed past a stack of AK-47s to receive our own. Sako showed us how to hold one. He set the gun down and looked over the smaller children in front of him. "Many of you are no taller than your guns. Is that not true?"

"Yes, Mon Lieutenant."

"And now," he told us, looking at me, so much larger than the other young captives, "I bring you God's word. Even the biggest of you is no taller than his gun. Say it! 'I am no taller than my gun!'"

"I am no taller than my gun!"

"One more time!" Sako said.

"I am no taller than my gun!"

"No churches, no crosses," Sako said. "That's not what matters. No schools. No parents. No priests, even. Just your gun. Say it! 'Just my gun!'"

"Just my gun!" the captives repeated.

"It is God's tool and God's will! Honor your gun, and you will be your own priest!"

That afternoon we went to the firing range. I watched a ten-year-old boy shoot his AK-47 at a humanlike target 30 meters away. The bullets kept missing the target, which was pulled by strings.

"Your turn, Lemba," Sako said.

I fired enough bullets into the target to cut off its head.

Sako grinned. "Excellent."

"I kill enough enemies," I asked, "I go back to Kinshasa?" How I missed Josiane and my café life!

"Not back to your father and mother?"

I said I missed them, too.

"Well," Sako said, "you're already with your family. We're it."

I said nothing.

"There's only one way to return to your mother and father," Sako said.

"How?" I asked.

"As a corpse."

I'd rather return alive, thank you, and I once again wondered what Josiane and my parents were thinking. Would my mysterious absence distract Josiane from her work? She was that kind of a sister. I could envision her dropping everything to look for me on the streets. My parents loved me just as much, but they were barely able to make it as it was. And what about Monsieur Zumbu? With me missing and Josiane preoccupied with finding me, his business would surely suffer. He himself was now almost like family, despite our initial wariness and his personal failings—what would he do without us?

Then my thoughts wandered back to Josiane. I could just imagine the conversation between Josiane and the police in some squalid station. She might go in a business suit bought especially for the occasion, just to impress the cops. "But you don't understand," she'd say. "He'd never go off on his own."

"Thousands are missing," a police officer would snap back. "You really expect us to stop the war to look for one teenaged boy?"

"100,000 francs to look for him?"

"Mademoiselle, I can't even begin to tell you how much it would cost."

Now, let me shift from conjecture into reality and tell of the horrors Josiane suffered, about which I would learn only indirectly and only later on. Thank God I was ignorant at the time.

6

CELLMATES, NOT ROOMMATES

MONSIEUR ZUMBU FROWNED at Josiane and looked at his watch. "Fifteen minutes late, and you're not even giving it your all."

"I sing my best," she said.

"When you're here," Monsieur Zumbu said. "All the customers, they ask, 'Where is Josiane? We want our song-bird *now*.'"

"But Monsieur, my brother's been gone for weeks now. Do you not have at least cousins? Can you not understand? I need time to look."

"However," Monsieur Zumbu said, as if she had not spoken at all, "I am a most flexible man."

"Flexible?" Josiane asked.

"You are now my employee. Suppose we really became friends."

"But Monsieur, I thought we were already friends."

Monsieur Zumbu reached to put his arm around her shoulder. "My sympathies over your brother."

Josiane broke away, spurning the advance my absence had encouraged.

That was enough for Josiane for the evening, but the worst actually happened just before closing, when Monsieur Zumbu said, "The time has come for a change in your duties. Follow me."

"Where to?" she asked.

"Just come with me, Josiane."

Monsieur Zumbu nudged her along to the back of the Internet Café, pulled out his bronze key and opened up the door, leading to some basement stairs.

"But Monsieur," she said, "I thought this area was private."

"Just follow me."

Josiane obliged. As she went down the stairs, she began to hear voices, although she couldn't make out what these people were saying or doing. Josiane and Monsieur Zumbu reached the bottom of stairs, where she saw cages stuffed with female sex slaves. Nearby was a room outfitted with plush couches and paintings of naked women. Josiane did not see any customers, but they would come in time through a tunnel leading to a building nearby. The brothel even took food deliveries from trusted merchants.

Monsieur Zumbu pointed toward the open doors of well-furnished rooms nearby. "These are your new duties." He gestured toward a cage containing two young women. "Meet your new roommates."

"But Monsieur, these are not roommates. These are cellmates."

"Do as you're told," he said, "and someday you may meet a rich appreciative man."

Josiane turned in the direction of the stairs, but Monsieur Zumbu grabbed her and began beating her, sparing her face, lest he damage the merchandise. He knew just how to slam his fist into her rear and other places where the bruises would most quickly fade away. Josiane screamed. Again and again he punched her just below her breasts, then in the stomach. Each blow alone wouldn't have been so painful, but all of them combined were. Josiane's yells would teach the other women and girls a useful lesson. I of course would have killed him on the spot had I been there. Just recalling what my dear sister went through makes me want to weep.

Beating done, Monsieur Zumbu unlocked a cage and shoved Josiane into it.

THE WHOLE TIME and for many months to come, I was blessedly unaware of my sister's fate. My own circumstances were about to change. Sako said someone wanted to meet me. That someone, it turned out, was Demon Killer, a muscular Purifier general huge enough to beat up two Tinys, or at least one and a half. Demon Killer had shown up at gun-worship ceremonies and was venerated as a founder of the Army. During the first months of my captivity, he had been away most of the time in other parts of the country, trying to spread the faith, or revolution, whatever you preferred to call it.

Little tattoos covered most of Demon Killer's forehead. On a left-hand finger, he wore a thick, oversized gold ring with an image of an AK-47 embossed into it. On a right-hand finger, a similar ring showed a rocket-propelled grenade launcher.

"Did we not promise you your own Little Airplane to fly?" Sako asked. "Bigger than your toy?"

I nodded. "But it still must be small and very fast—hard to shoot down."

"Yes!" said Tiny. "Eyes in the sky to help slay God's enemies! And Demon Killer can help you get it."

"Glad to meet you, Lemba," Demon Killer said. "You can call me 'Killer' for short. If you dare."

"Please," I said, "take me back to Kinshasa."

"That's where we're going," Demon Killer said. And so we ended up in Kinshasa at Hanno's Technology Store. Of course, the whole time back in the capital, I was wondering if I could run away and find Josiane or get her a message of some kind. But I knew that Demon Killer would be keeping too close an eye on me. The best I could manage was to stay calm and try to loosen him up with small talk.

"How many demons have you killed, Mon Général?" I asked him.

Demon Killer eagerly pointed to the stars, circles, and dots on his forehead. "Enemies slain. I'm already running out of room. My AK and machete, we are truly blessed."

I gazed some more at Demon Killer's forehead. "Your marks...how come some are stars, and some are circles, and some are..."

"The stars, they represent tens of enemies."

"And the circles?"

"Hundreds."

I couldn't help raising an eyebrow.

"It's God's truth," Demon Killer said. "Honor your gun and everything is possible." Pause. "You didn't ask me about the smaller dots."

"What about the dots?"

"Demons I killed one by one. Now, about my rings." Demon Killer held up his hands. I once again took in the sight of the two rings emblazoned with images of beloved weapons.

"The AK's my favorite ring. But never look down on the RPG. God loves them both."

"Your real AK," I asked, "does it have a name?"

"Big Demon Killer."

"But surely you are taller."

"Not in the eyes of God. No man is taller than his gun."

Back at the camp, I immediately began assembling the newly bought quadcopter, a fancier, bigger version of the one I'd purchased for my act at Pierre's Internet Café.

"Young soldier," Demon Killer said, "I'm proud of you. Tell me. Someday we buy you one able to carry bombs?"

"Bombs?" I said. "Maybe small ones, yes. We can always log on to DarkMarket."

"DarkMarket? It's not Satanic, is it?"

"Just a place online to buy stuff. Drones...bombs...poison gas." I knew the basic lore. The authorities had shut down DarkMarket, only for it to revive itself in time, better protected than ever by crypto technology.

"That's not Satanic," Demon Killer said. "That's angelic."

"I do what you want, you let me go?" Of course, I wanted my freedom back in Kinshasa to be with Josiane. But Demon Killer was fixated on another idea—a comparison between his Mighty Warrior self and my parents.

"What a foolish boy. Could your parents buy you drones? Useless. I kill them, maybe you pay more attention to me."

Prudently I avoided a comeback.

I fiddled with the assembled quadcopter drone. Suddenly, shells start falling all around us. A loud buzzer sounded, and Tiny got on the PA system. "Everyone to their stations!"

Soldiers dashed out, and in no time at all, the Purifier artillery was firing back.

Enemy shells came terrifyingly close, but Tiny's soldiers successfully repelled the attackers with their own artillery and rocket-propelled grenades.

Back at the drill grounds, near the newly constructed drone hut, I gazed at the blackened remains of the quad-copter, destroyed in the attack. I didn't like how the Purifiers intended to use the drones, but as a true gadgeteer, I couldn't hide my sadness over the fate of my bigger, better toy.

"It is okay," Demon Killer said. "We'll go back to Kinshasa and find another."

Tiny frowned. "No! God has spoken—God says to wait!"

"Not exactly," said Demon Killer. "He wants Lemba to fly his Little Airplane."

"But," Tiny asked, still caught up in his practical theology, "what if God instead created Lemba to fire his AK? No one does it better. A divine gift!"

No! My gift was as a brother and tech guru. How I longed to be back with Josiane at the Internet Café. If I had to choose, I'd pick drones and video games over guns any time. I didn't want to kill, just satiate my gadget lust.

DEMON KILLER COULDN'T DECIDE whether to treat me as a captive, a son, or both. During our first time together in a Purifier tent, he'd invited me for a meal of goat's meat. Almost the whole time we were waiting for an aide to serve us, he was tenderly stroking his pistol barrel.

When I asked about the object of his affections, he said: "This is my family now. The more I use it, the closer I am to God. What are guns but part of His holiness?"

That spooked me, and Demon Killer must have noticed my slight quivers.

"No, no, don't fear," he said. "You'll never be fish food, unless..."

"Unless?"

"Unless I kill you. But as long as you obey..."

"Oui, Mon Général."

"You and your Little Airplanes," said Demon Killer, slipping back into his full paternal mood, "are like me and my motorboats."

"You grew up by a river?" I asked. "Yes? Me, too."

"By the sea. I get around," he said. "Boat engines, bicycles, trucks, anything with gears. I've always been the smartest."

I dutifully nodded.

"God loves machinery," Demon Killer went on. "He loves guns. He loves your Little Airplanes. Kill enough devils with them, and we'll be brothers in heaven. Defy me, and the fish will feast on you."

7

————

LET TINY AND SAKO
LOSE THEIR OWN ARMS

BULLETS WHIZZED toward us from a ridge above as we hid in the thick shrubbery below. Then the shooting stopped.

I had killed a government sniper with my AK-47. He had been a short, mustachioed man in his early 30s who looked too frail to be a soldier. I hadn't any doubt I would have prevailed in hand-to-hand combat.

My bullets had shattered his face, but I imagined it as a kind face whose last expression had shown mild surprise. I wondered if he was a father with a boy my age. Then I started thinking of him, too, as a son, brother, and nephew whose family would miss him just as much as mine would miss me. I had irrevocably scarred the lives and happiness of those dear to him.

By chance, might he himself be a twin with a sister with whom he shared a triangle-shaped birthmark in the same place? I doubted it. But when you're just 15, you're more likely to see others in such idiosyncratic ways. I could imagine Josiane, in my place, thinking similar thoughts on families and killing.

This was the first time I'd gunned down a living,

breathing human, not a feelingless avatar in a video game. I remembered a sermon from our village priest. Killing was acceptable only in "just" wars. This one did not qualify. It was not a genuine war, rather a despicable series of criminal acts driven by greed and delusion. Now I was among the perpetrators. True, the Purifiers had threatened to kill me if I did not live up to my marksmanship on the practice firing range. But I still felt queasy. This was different from hunting for bushmeat for family dinner. I'd yet to evolve to my potential as a truly compassionate human being, but at least I had started.

Lieutenant Vomit Tooth had himself killed two government soldiers. "See," he bragged to me as we searched the bodies for cigarettes and other prizes, "you're not the only master marksman." Pathetic. Sako must have spent years at this but was still comparing himself to a 15-year-old boy.

Sako then did unspeakable things to the corpses, details I'll not share, and turned to the 13-year-old beside him.

"Honor your gun!" Sako said, gesturing toward the bodies. "Fire it at the scum!"

The boy hesitated. The government soldiers were already as dead as could be.

"Plenty of bullets left," Sako said. "It'll make you more comfortable killing the live ones. Do your new family proud. Remember, we're all you've got now."

The 13-year-old was Mpasi, the boy I would go on both to protect and hate, and in time he would become one of the more enthusiastic child soldiers, never missing a chance to please his "new family," despite the horrors committed against his old one. It was as though, by fully embracing the present, Mpasi could better forget the past, even the massacre of his parents. But that would come later. For now, he still dreamed of an escape.

Regardless of the atrocities around us, Mpasi at times could still act like any 13-year-old. I remember the times we kicked around a "football" made of twigs and leaves, tied together with string.

"Yes," I said, "score one for you!"

"Our team," Mpasi said. "Undefeated!"

I laughed. We might yet make it to our make-believe World Cup. And then, out of the blue, I recalled a question I'd been meaning to ask him. "Did I hear you say you were from Sambuka?"

Mpasi nodded.

"And me," I said, "I'm from Zange. Neighbors, almost. Know that bend of the river? We're right near the tip."

The next day, football and our childhoods couldn't have been farther from our minds. The Purifiers had burned down yet another village, one of the hundreds they leveled, and they gleefully lined up the inhabitants for executions.

"Government supporters, all of them!" Sako said, fists shaking.

"How do you know?" I was tempted to ask. "What are you doing, keeping files?" But I sensibly kept my curiosity in check.

Sako turned to Mpasi. "The time has come to show your manhood again." Sako reached down to point Mpasi's AK-47 at a wiry man in his thirties and his tiny wife and three young children. "Go ahead, kill them! Be a soldier."

"But I'm just a farmer," the man said before Mpasi could shoot. "I have nothing to do with the Kinshasa. Why, I don't even pay my taxes."

"Enough of your lies!" Sako said.

The man and his wife tightly held hands and looked at each other. The children clung to both of them.

If I'd been in Mpasi's place, Sako would have had to say

to me: "Do it or we'll come back to kill all your uncles." But without delay, Mpasi's thin little finger pressed the trigger again and again until the family was dead.

"I'm proud of you," Sako said, patting Mpasi on the head. "You have truly honored your gun."

TINY AND SAKO never missed an opportunity to imbue their troops, young and old, with as much cruelty as the two could manage. One day, Tiny gathered his soldiers to introduce them to a beautiful twentyish woman in a short-sleeved cotton print dress. Her right arm was missing.

"Do you want to know why we fight?" Tiny said. "Ask my niece. Makinu, tell them how you lost the arm."

"The Kia Tribe," she said.

"Yes," said Tiny, "the very allies of the government. And they say we are the barbarians? But you haven't heard the rest of it. Makinu, tell them what the Kias did after they cut off your arm."

"Then they made me watch them eat it. And next time they say—next time, they come for my husband's heart."

"Cannibals," said Tiny, shaking his fist. "*That* is who we fight!"

I felt sorry for Makinu, who, under other circumstances, might have been my sister—anyone's sister. But the whole revolting spectacle made me all the more eager to escape. I didn't even belong to Tiny's tribe. Why should I reciprocate with barbarities of my own?

Out of my pocket, later that day, I pulled the photo of me with Josiane and my parents. What better inspiration! Perhaps I could just walk away. Screw the risks. No Kia-fighting for me. Let Tiny and Sako lose their own arms. And why should I help a crook like Tiny grab oil or mineral wealth? He was probably not that eager to share the loot, as if my part of it would be more than a speck anyway.

The Purifiers' camp was some 155 kilometers from Kinshasa. I remembered the way back to the capital from my drone-shopping trip with Demon Killer, and once there I could talk Monsieur Zumbu into lending me the money for a bus trip back to my parents' village. I'd lie low near Zange for a while, then maybe look for a job in an establishment where the Purifiers would be less likely to be searching for me. Regardless of my special talents, did they really care about a 15-year-old? I asked Mpasi if he wanted to come along, and he said he would. He at least had uncles to return to.

I snuck into the tent where the Purifiers stored fruit slices, bread, peanut butter, and other fare that could fuel my travels. No one was supposed to be around at this time. But somebody was, the pimple-faced soldier. He asked what I wanted the food for.

"Tiny's niece," I said out of the blue. "She's having a birthday party. Just here to try out the food."

"*I'm* the one who handles this."

Oh, well, Mpasi and I could make do with berries and stolen bananas and other odds and ends. And so, that night, we just snuck off—silently and into the bushes, so as not to be spotted by the camp guards, who were looking anyway in the other direction.

Nearby we could hear hyena barks. I started thinking of all the interesting ways to die in the Congo without help from the Purifiers—puff adder snakes, crocodiles, malarial mosquitoes, maybe even a stray lion or leopard, although I didn't expect to run across that many big cats. Still, you never knew. Lions at times feasted on baby crocs, and crocodiles were known to return the favor by attacking lions drinking from lakes and ponds.

By dawn, walking along the dusty roads, Mpasi and I had covered a good 40 kilometers. The temperature must have reached 35 degrees Celsius, and we were sweating in our Purifier uniforms, from which we'd ripped off the insignias.

We tried to wave down a ride. But the few motorists we saw just sped past us. Mpasi and I kept up our spirits by dreaming of what our free selves would do. Most of all, Mpasi simply wanted to go hunting and fishing with his uncles, who he hoped would buy him a cellphone.

Number one on my list would be a quick check-in with Monsieur Zumbu and my sister. I prayed that the news would be good—that all the talent scouts in Kinshasa had watched Josiane on television and decided she was ready for a major recording contract. About my parents, I simply hoped that they were safe, their crops were faring well, and no one had stolen their new oversized TV. Of course, I had mixed feelings about returning permanently to my parents' home—exactly the kind of place where the Purifiers might be most likely to look for me. It was one more reason why I wanted to be instead with my beloved sister, even if, in the interest of safety, I might also have to avoid the Internet Café most of the time.

A green truck with a canopy rumbled by. Then it backed up. Two men climbed out of the cab, and Mpasi and I ran for our lives, only to be caught.

"Haven't I seen you before?" one asked. "You're Purifiers, aren't you?"

"No," I said.

"Not government?"

I shook my head.

"You'd better not be," he said, "because we're Purifiers, too."

"Too?"

"Yes," he said, "I *have* seen you."

Then the men started tying Mpasi and me up.

"That'll teach you," our first captor said. "Once a Purifier, always a Purifier. Dead or alive."

"Dead most likely," said the second. "Either way, a reward for us."

I remembered the fool-talk I'd heard in training camp. "Oh, good," I mocked the Purifiers, "maybe I can get to Heaven and eat cake with the other boys."

"Not if you escaped."

8

THE GALLOWS

BACK AT THE PURIFIER CAMP, my captors had tied Mpasi and me to stakes on a wooden platform. Tiny whipped me in front of dozens of soldiers, while Sako took care of Mpasi. Helpfully, the Purifiers had modified the platform to do double duty as a gallows.

I would have favored a firing squad—let them get it over in a flash with their trusty AK-47s. One month before, I'd watched the Purifiers botch a hanging of a government military officer. The rotten rope wasn't strong enough, so the man fell to the platform with his neck not entirely snapped. Blood spurted from his head as he twitched. It took a while to fetch a second rope and repeat the hanging for him to die. I'd even have preferred getting my head split open with a nice, clean machete cut, which, like the AK-47 executions, was well within the Purifiers' skill set.

Pondering my ultimate destination, I doubted I would be eating cakes and mating with nubile ladies to produce football stars. I'd settle instead for calm, star-filled celestial surroundings where I could await the coming of my parents and sister while listening to all the rumba music and other heavenly sounds I desired.

Ideally, God could summon up some tracks by Petit-Pays, and if I also could watch YouTubes and Nigerian action movies, so much the better. Maybe I could even play video games with companionable angels.

And then I started distracting myself with more realistic thoughts—of Josiane, of her singing and dancing in talent competitions, of my parents caught up in their favorite TV drama. Not to neglect Kodjo. I tried to imagine our dear pet feasting on river rats—far from our shack, of course—or enjoying whatever else made him happiest beyond playing with me and the rest of us.

"WE TRUSTED YOU," Tiny screamed at us there on the platform. "We shared our guns with you." *Lash.* "We bring you closer to God. And you? You just wander off like the ungrateful infidel you are."

In the crowd below, Demon Killer watched his young involuntary protégé being whipped. I'd like to think he wasn't enjoying the sight. He didn't impress me exactly as the most caring and sensitive soul. But if nothing else, if Tiny in the future let him use drones, he would have to search for another expert in Little Airplanes to replace me.

"The shame of it all," Tiny said. "To desert is to bend before the Kias." Still more lashes. Then Tiny turned to the crowd. "We will now get on with the hanging."

I would be first. Tiny slipped a noose around my neck and tightened it. I couldn't see Mpasi, but he must have been trembling. Tiny was about to kick the stool out from under my feet. Then, abruptly, he stopped.

"Wait!" Tiny said. "Our God is a merciful one, and He has just spoken to me. You will not be hanged now."

"*Merci*, Mon Général!" I said.

"Instead," Tiny said, "I'll give you the privilege of carrying out God's will."

Why this change of heart? Just what did he mean? But I was pleased enough—Heaven could wait.

"Take the noose off," Tiny told Sako, who did. Tiny turned to me. "Don't get too smug. We might need it."

Sako and others brought Mpasi and me, both in hand-cuffs, to Tiny's shack. Waving everyone else away, including me, Tiny said, "I want a few words with Mpasi. Five minutes and you can bring Lemba back." So we left. But even from 15 meters away we could hear loud unintelligible chants from Tiny coming through the walls of his shack. Would we die after all? Still cuffed and watched over by Sako, I paced nervously.

Finally, Tiny opened the door and a dazed-looking Mpasi came out. "Mpasi," he said with me within easy intimidation distance, "for you it is clear. Straight to the gallows if you ever desert again."

Mpasi nodded.

Tiny gestured toward me, Sako unlocked the cuffs, and I joined the chief Purifier in the shack.

"You, Lemba, the same—death if you even think of walking away," Tiny said as I sat down on a fold-up wooden chair uncomfortable enough to be just another form of torture. "You even *think* about deserting, and my gun will tell me. And now a special opportunity. Prove your loyalty. Do what you should have done in the first place."

"And what is that, Mon Général?"

"A leader is not a leader unless he leads by action," Tiny said. "I don't hide behind others. My plans are my deeds."

"What are you saying?" I asked

"We know where you're from and where your parents live."

"No! Please no." I feared for my mother and father but was grateful that Tiny hadn't mentioned Josiane.

"Cleanse yourself, Lemba. Honor your God, your gun, and the Purification Army."

"Better to honor my family!"

"Kill your parents, or we'll kill you. Tomorrow, you and I leave for Zange."

"I'll kill myself first."

"Only if you get a chance. We'll do to you what the Kias did to my beloved niece. *Then* kill you. You agree?"

"Let me think about it."

"No! Answer—now!"

I sobbed. Tiny put his arm around me, as if to offer comfort.

"What are you," he said, "but a child in need of purification? You're right-handed, aren't you?"

I said yes.

"So," Tiny said, "that's the arm we'll chop off first."

"But doesn't 'purification' mean death?"

"That's what you prefer, right? I can tell, and my gun agrees."

"What if I do kill my parents?"

"You would?" Tiny asked in genuine surprise, having already known what a difficult case I was.

I, of course, hadn't the least intention of letting my parents or me go to Heaven right now, either separately or together.

The odds were still scary, but I could try to buy time.

～

"You won't change your mind, will you?" Sako asked me as our unmarked Purifier car neared Zange.

"God's will," I said. "How can I fight it? But what to tell my parents?"

"Tell them that the Purification Army is your new family."

"I don't understand how you know so much about them."

"God's eyes are everywhere," Tiny said. "You don't think we've researched you? Who do you think we are, half-witted barbarians? You and your machines. You think you're so much better than we are."

"*Mon Dieu*, of course not," I lied.

"That's better." Tiny just might have been enough of a narcissist to believe me.

Arrived at my family's shack, I knocked on the door, with Tiny and Sako nearby. Sako for now was the one carrying the AK-47. They already were smiling widely as if preparing to put their victims at ease. My parents glowed with happiness at the sight of me. Through the opened door I could see the customary midday meal on the scratched-up old dining table. Our dog, Kodjo, was nearby, chomping energetically on a carrot. He looked up and rushed over to my feet. No doubt about it: he'd missed me. Badly. I could barely resist the urge to ignore the Purifiers and pet him.

"Lemba!" Papa said, arms open for a hug, and I obliged.

"Oh, my son," Mama said, "we thought you were dead. A miracle!"

"Who are your friends?" Papa asked.

"This is Général Lula," I said, "and Lieutenant Tota."

Tiny and Sako keep beaming at the older Adulas.

"I have good news," I said. "I've joined the Congolese Purification Army. I'm a Purifier all the way! Head to toe."

"But," Mama asked, "how could you—"

"They're my new family," I said, looking in my parents' direction and with as much of a wink as I could summon up.

Sako handed me the AK-47 and rested a knife blade against my neck with one hand. Tiny kept the AK-47 pointed at Mama and Papa.

"But if they are your new family," Papa asked, "why the gun and knife?"

"Because," I shouted with all the sincerity I could feign, "it is GOD'S WILL!"

My passionate yell had just the right effect on Tiny and Sako, causing them to relax their guard so I could use my martial-arts magic against them.

With a mighty move and an uppercut of my left elbow, I knocked the knife at my neck from Sako's hand.

I spun around at the same time with the AK-47 in my right hand, already pressing the trigger to tear into Tiny and Sako with a swath of bullets at chest height. I killed Tiny, but Sako at first eluded me while I was focused on the General. But then Kodjo hurled himself at Sako, sinking his teeth into his thigh, distracting him long enough for me to fire a full arc of the AK-47 bullets across the lieutenant's chest and stomach. I didn't merely take out Tiny and Sako. I kept pumping bullets into them to see if I could kill their demonic souls along with their bodies.

The blood was red. But if it had been green, I wouldn't have been surprised—that's how different they seemed to me at the time from the rest of the human race.

I'd felt nauseous while killing enemy soldiers and innocent villagers under Sako's watchful eyes, as well I should have, given my moral upbringing, to which my old village priest had contributed. But *this* bloodshed was cause for celebration.

Are you shocked that a mere teenager could feel this way? Please don't be. The survival of my parents mattered to me far more than the deaths of Tiny and Sako.

"I like my old family better," I told Mama and Papa with a wide grin and rushed forward to hug them. "So safe, so safe. So happy to be home."

"Praise God, praise Jesus," Mama said, gazing down at the riddled corpses. "What evil men!"

"The whole time," I said, "I could think of nothing but being able to see you and Papa again. Josiane, too."

"If only God will let *us* see her."

"She's missing?" We were that close a family—I could think of no other possibility.

"We take the bus to Kinshasa," Mama said, "and see the man in the café."

Papa threw up his hands. "Nothing. He just says she vanished—"

"—while searching for you," Mama added.

My loving twin sister! That would have been so much in character for Josiane. The least I could do in return was to start searching for *her*.

We all looked down again at the dead bodies lying on the floor in blood. "I think we've got some cleanup to do," Papa said.

"Not a word to the police," I said. "We don't want word to get out faster than it has to."

We waited until night to take care of the bodies, which we loaded into an old cart. Poor Papa. I bore as much of Tiny's weight as I could, but it was still back-breaking work, and I worried that Papa would injure himself helping me. We disposed of the Purifier car by stripping it of license tags and pushing it into the river.

"Maybe," I told Papa, "you and Mama should stay with Uncle Balingi until it's safer." Let me hasten to add that the "Uncle" was an honorific.

"But this is our home."

"Just promise me," I said, "that you will keep the guns. Their friends come by, you kill them."

9

A BUILT-IN GPS FOR SLEAZE

I KEPT my promise to Mama, Papa, and myself. All over Kinshasa, I asked about Josiane while hoping that the Purifiers would not catch wind of my own whereabouts. I disguised myself in a halfhearted way with sunglasses. I even checked the police stations, actually among the more dangerous places, given the ease with which the Purifiers in the past had bribed the cops in Kinshasa.

At the Internet Café, a startled Monsieur Zumbu embraced me and said how sorry he was about Josiane. "I cry with sadness. The customers—they can't stop talking about her. Five girls I've tried. None as good! I can imagine how hard this must be on your parents. First you go missing, and then Josiane does."

I nodded, and Monsieur Zumbu put a comforting arm on my shoulder. "How would you like your old job back?" he asked.

"But what if the Purifiers see me here?"

"Not to worry. I haven't seen any Purifiers in months."

"But this is the first place they'd look for me."

"I bet they think you're too smart to return here," Monsieur Zumbu said.

"Maybe I am."

He laughed. "I can't tell you how much the customers miss you. You want a raise? Just name the amount. No Lemba, no Josiane, I could go out of business."

I would be gambling my life if I returned, but I needed the money, and, flaws aside, Monsieur Zumbu had treated me like a son. So I went back. Even then I knew my Achilles heel—being too nice at times to those close to me. But so be it. I re-immersed myself in the Internet and the related technology, educating myself further through YouTube and other means, flying toy drones, DJing, glad-handing customers.

On my off days, joined at times by a few of her most ardent fans, I resumed my search for Josiane. Our love and closeness made the disappearance all the scarier. I just could not imagine her running away and leaving my parents and me in the dark. Something foul must have happened. Of course, in this memoir I've already given away *part* of the story. Now imagine what I was imagining when I learned she was gone. Was she at the bottom of the Congo River? Maybe working the streets of Kinshasa as a young prostitute with an attentive pimp nearby to keep her in line? I already knew enough about street life to understand how rapidly such a trade could age young women. I envisioned her with a prematurely lined face and the sparkle stolen from her eyes. How I worried!

I'd done all I could with my wanderings from police station to police station, hospital to hospital, brothel to brothel. But I had an idea. Maybe Doka the Fixer could help. He had a built-in GPS for sleaze. If something shady was afoot, Doka could find his way to it and turn a profit.

To my surprise, another slimeball was living in Doka's shack. I asked where Doka was now.

"He's got himself a nice place in Prosperity City." That was the name of a gated Kinshasa real estate development for the rich and would-be rich along the Congo River.

"How did that happen?"

"Doka's on the computer now," the new slimeball said.

After a little more questioning, I ascertained that Doka overnight had transmogrified himself from a garden-variety street hustler to a YouTube star with a hefty hit count. I called up his show when I got back to the Internet Café. The title was misleadingly bland, "Kin Nightlife Plus-Plus." On the actual program, Doka showed hookers strutting around, and he offered tips for interested tourists on how not to be mugged or—get this!—pickpocketed. He knew all the geographical subtleties of life in the local red-light areas. Stay on this street, if you're alone. That street is fine if friends are with you. And no—don't venture on this other street even if accompanied by armed bodyguards. Go to such-and-such street instead. Just want to look? Well, here's where all the women always wear skimpy swimsuits. Interested in under-aged hookers with a little more covering? On such and such streets you can patronize teenaged girls wearing 1960ish miniskirts.

Via the Web I found Doka's phone number and asked if I could drop by to discuss employment opportunities. I told him how I'd reinvented myself, too. Of course, I hadn't the least interest in working for Doka permanently, given my abhorrence of him and his trade. On YouTube, many of the prostitutes he showed looked young enough to be *udjana* girls, Kinshasa street slang for under-aged urban sex workers. Past governments in Kin might have put such a brazen pimp out of business or come close to it, but not one distracted by a civil war in the vicinity. I worried that Josiane was now a *udjana*. Please, no!

Doka lived on the second floor of a just-built walkup with palm trees in front. He greeted me at the door as if he actually wanted to see me. Doka no longer looked quite so pimpy—he'd refined his bizarreness. Instead he was dressed like a sapeur, a dandy, complete with a bright orange tie, a striped blue shirt, and a purple suit. No rules crimped sapeur fashion. He could just as well have been wearing kilts.

Squinting at me with his gimlet eyes, he asked about my database skills, which he could use in marketing and in matching clients with prostitutes of either sex. He was expanding and needed help—the existing database guy had died in a boating accident.

Doka also was still plying his trade as a fixer at large. He was even serving as a bagman for the Congolese Purification Army. "You want to bribe someone, I'm the best. Cash, drugs, women, or men—I know what works."

I was amazed how open he was. Perhaps Doka was sufficiently full of himself to believe that I would go to work for him for certain. I would have received several times what Monsieur Zumbu was paying. I heard the whole pitch, taking care not to raise an eyebrow on mention of the Purifiers.

"So what do you think, Lemba?" Doka asked. "Are you ready to grow?" He might as well have been a corporate recruiter.

I was touched by his trust. Remember, I was only 15—well, about to turn 16 after my time with the Purifiers—and it wasn't as if he'd tested my database skills. But I really had them or at least could fake the missing parts until I did. Maybe I could work for him long enough part-time to see if Josiane's name popped up in one of the databases.

"I need an answer," Doka said.

"And I need to think this over," I stalled.

"This can't wait," he said. "You can't make up your mind, you're the wrong person for the job."

"I still—"

"Get out!" Doka angrily pointed to the door. "Go back to pickpocketing."

10

———

"YOU BETRAY ME, I'LL
SNAP YOUR NECK"

Listening to the radio one day as I surfed the Web, I heard a newsreader tell of "a change of leadership rumored to have occurred within the Congolese Purification Army." I could speculate but would rather not think any more of those abhorrent people. I started looking ahead and mulling over my future, not my past.

What if I could jet off to Canada or America, US racists notwithstanding, and even figure out a way to fly my parents there in time?

This all seemed such a far-fetched dream, but others had lived it out. I loved my village, but not the violence—how I wanted our family to escape! If only Josiane could suddenly reappear at the last minute at the airport and join us! I wouldn't leave the Congo directly. First maybe I could bag down a job at one of the French, American, Chinese, or other foreign tech companies that were expanding offices in Kinshasa despite the putrid government and threats like the Purifiers. Most of these imported corporate types wouldn't stay long amid all the violence. They wanted locals to take over. Who better qualified than me? From Java to user experience and advanced Web site design and Search Engine Optimization, I set out to educate myself and be the best.

Walking along the streets one evening, I spotted two bulky men trailing me. I sped up, and they did, too. I turned a corner and darted into an alley, but they followed and trapped me. "OK," I said, 100 percent certain they were Purifiers, "let's get it over with." This appointment at the gallows would be my last.

One of the men laughed. "Please, Lemba, we're not here to kill you. We're here to reunite you."

They escorted me to a nondescript office building and opened up a door to an office on the tenth floor. And there, awaiting us, was none other than Demon Killer, all 220 centimeters of him, eating a takeout meal of chicken, beans, and rice.

"Demon Killer! What are you doing here?"

"To bring you home," he said.

Had Doka had anything to do with this? I decided not to gamble by asking Demon Killer.

"Home is where my dear ones are," I said.

"You haven't heard? I'm the new Chief! The Général of all Générals, with a little help from my AK!"

"Quite a promotion!" I said with all the enthusiasm I could fake. "What about Tiny?"

"God loves His Little Airplanes, and Tiny got in the way. God wants you to fly them. Lemba, come back. You're our lucky airplane child."

"Back to those who would kill my parents?" I instantly hated myself for bringing up Mama and Papa and reminding him of my vulnerability. But it was too late.

"*That* was Tiny and Sako." He pointed to himself. "*This* is Demon Killer. No one messes with God. No one messes with Demon Killer. It's a new day for the Purification Army."

"So my parents will be safe?" I wanted to ask. I didn't. But Demon Killer more or less finished my thought for me.

"Are your parents Kias?"

I shook my head.

"Then they have nothing to fear...if you do what I say."

Demon Killer pulled out a photo of Mama and Papa working their fields. "How'd you like some protection for them? I send one of my men to spread the word. Lemba's parents are safe!"

"But can I believe you?"

"If you and your parents want to live. You betray me, I snap your neck." Demon Killer demonstrated with a chicken bone from the takeout meal. "Or maybe slit your throats." He made exactly the right slitting sound and, with an extended finger, did a knife act on his throat. "Just like a chicken."

I recoiled.

"I kill your dog, too."

So he even knew, somehow, about Kodjo? This threat was all too real.

"Oh, come on," Demon Killer said. "Let's be friends. I'd rather not do what I'd have to do. And you...from now on, you can just call me 'Killer' if you want!"

I nodded.

"But you double-cross me," he said, "I live up to my name."

Demon Killer made another throat-slitting sound, this time also using his knife to attack his vegetables.

I knew I hadn't any choice if I wanted to evade the fates of the chicken and the cucumbers.

In Kinshasa and on the trip back to the Purifier camp, Demon Killer filled me in on the details of the "change of leadership" reported on the radio.

Demon Killer lied and said he'd AKed Tiny and Sako out of the way—I modestly kept quiet about the true cause of their demise. No, he never broached the possibility of my having killed them. He was too much in love with his own story—that *he* had cleared the way for his new glory as leader of the Purifiers.

Tiny and Sako's allies had survived. So Demon Killer's faction finished off the biggest threats with machetes and public head-splittings.

"What a shame," Demon Killer told me. "Both friends. But you do what you need to do."

Friends? Could Demon Killer really have had any? What he meant to say was "useful people." As a teenager, I couldn't fathom all the nuances of relationships, but even then, I understood. I wanted to survive. How could I be "useful" and stay alive without becoming a monster?

"The sad thing is that we are all victims," Demon Killer said. "That is what Tiny and I had in common." And it was then, perhaps to bond with me in a utilitarian way, that Demon Killer spilled out his personal history and the story of the Purifiers. He skipped over his real name along with a few other touchy details, but I fully understood. "Demon Killer" made him seem closer to his gun and God.

I already knew how much the Purification Army loved guns and hated organized religion, especially the Catholic Church, and the other motives were obvious. The greed. The power-lust. And, yes, the same hatred that all of us Congolese shared toward the old colonials who had stolen our freedom and wealth. The exploitation in more subtle forms went on, but that by itself would hardly explain his bizarre theology.

Demon Killer confided more on the origins of both himself and his gun worship. He came from a family of fishermen and truck drivers. Thanks to the latter trade, he had inland relatives far beyond the oceanside village of his birth —along with the accompanying tribal feuds, especially with the tribe known as the Kias. Both Demon Killer's relatives and the Kias had long forgotten the origins of the feuds. But they kept up their grudges, as natural to them as breathing or burning down a village. His parents were drunks and worse—his father treated him in the vilest of ways like a woman; so, expecting relief, the boy blurted out his plight to a rogue village priest, Père Banza.

The Catholic Church had cast Père Banza off for proclaiming himself the equal of Jesus, a theological subtlety lost to his worshipful, half-educated flock. The priest had stopped the abuse with a holy threat against Demon Killer's father.

Grateful, Demon Killer joined him in prayer to give thanks, after which his supposed savior reached for the boy's privates. Now Père Banza could continue the abominations himself, sharing young Demon Killer with no one. "*That*," said the priest, "is what I've thanked God for."

Demon Killer ran back home, grabbed his father's hunting rifle, and returned to the church to shoot Père Banza dead. Then he stole cash from the priest's office so that the village might dismiss the killing as a mere robbery. An altar boy like Demon Killer would have seemed the least likely suspect even without such a precaution.

His father never raped Demon Killer again. He correctly surmised that the boy would be just as likely to kill him.

"So now you know," Demon Killer said, "how I learned

the godliness of guns. Did the priest save me in the end? No! Did the church? No, just a gun. Forget the cross, forget the crucifix. Only a gun can protect you."

As a devout Catholic, I was repulsed. Père Kasongo cared just as much about my schoolhouse—so dear to my family and the others in our village—as he did about our wooden church. Remember, he was our village leader as well as our priest. At times he even helped Papa and others in the fields without asking anything in return. I wanted to argue back with Demon Killer but wisely refrained.

Demon Killer told me the rest of his story. Shortly after he became a truck driver in his early 20s, a woman caught his eye at a bar. There was a problem in the form of her boyfriend, Tiny. Demon Killer beat him bloody—no small feat since Tiny was a near-giant. The woman agreed to be Demon Killer's. But she had a request. They should take care of Tiny while he recovered from his wounds. Demon Killer reluctantly agreed—very much to his happiness in the end, for the two men had plenty in common. They shared tribal connections and a related hatred of the Kias, along with similar histories of fatherly abuse. Demon Killer and Tiny even started a trucking line together in time, intimidating rivals in every possible way, especially head-cracking. As I've said, Demon Killer was immune to genuine friendship but endlessly capable of cultivating useful people.

One day, Demon Killer's woman died under the wheel of a luxury car driven by the owner of a plantation that grew rare plants for Western pharmaceutical companies. Demon Killer rushed to the mansion to kill him. Instead, based on the trucker's local fame as a successful thug, the two men struck a business deal. The plantation owner hated paying taxes to the Kinshasa government even if some of the money found itself into hands of family members working in the capital. Why not hire Demon Killer and Tiny to start a rebellion against the central government and its tax collectors? Maybe the fighting could spread to the whole country, and the Purifiers would win. Then the plantation owner's rich friends and loved ones could steal yet more with full control of Kinshasa.

"Our investors"—that is what Demon Killer called the plantation owner and the others. Under normal circumstances, those backers would have held the upper hand. Not so with Demon Killer and Tiny. Yes, they were just semi-educated. But by way of blackmail and machetes and AK-47s —not to mention discreet cash from Rwanda and Uganda, out to grab Congolese minerals amid the chaos—the two prevailed over the original "investors." I learned those extra tidbits and more from newspaper articles some years later.

The foreign money men favored Tiny as Purifier leader because he was a little less of a whack job. Besides, Demon Killer was often away in Kinshasa or the eastern part of the Democratic Republic of the Congo, engaged in "business development," as he called it—notably, the fomenting of more revolution in places of most interest to Rwanda and Uganda.

All along, Tiny and Demon Killer delivered tirade after tirade against the very foreigners who secretly funded them, until the pair grew too crazy to be useful even as chaos-multipliers.

Though Demon Killer didn't level with me about the foreigners, he made it clear that *he* was the creator of the sacred gun-worship rituals that held the Purifiers together. What a mistake—letting Tiny lead! But Demon Killer had bided his time. And now his gun had rewarded him for his patience. Demon Killer was not always the brightest man, of course, but he could be a genius at homing in on the weaknesses of those he wished to destroy or manipulate, including me—with all my fears over my parents. All too often, alas, on top of everything else, the Almighty had been fickle enough to reward him with an outsized share of luck.

Demon Killer also told me about Sako. Despite the man's bad teeth, the lieutenant hadn't fared that badly in the past as an overseer on the first "investor's" plantation. In the business deal struck after the automobile accident, one condition was that Sako would be the backers' man on the scene and help keep tabs on Demon Killer and Tiny. Sako started out as a colonel in the Purification Army, diminishing in rank as the two other men's power over the original investors grew. Still, Demon Killer and Tiny had paid him enough to keep him in line.

I took it for granted that Demon Killer might be inventing and exaggerating. But even if just partially true, his words sufficed to encourage caution.

Once again, I remembered the glee with which Demon Killer snapped that chicken bone.

Via a satellite phone back at the camp, I called my parents. Sparing them all the details, I told of my return to the Purification Army. "But why are you back with them?" Papa asked.

"They said they'd kill us all."

"I guess we'll have to move," Papa sighed.

"Not so fast," I said. "I do what they want, they say they'll protect you." I explained about the guard that Demon Killer promised to send. "Big fellow—he's handy with a machete." His name was Bota, and although just a teenager, he stood almost two meters tall and had helped Tiny with many head-splittings.

"Will you call again soon?" Papa asked.

"When I can," I said. "Oh, and Bota can double as a field hand."

"I could use the help."

"You've still got those guns?" I asked.

"I go to sleep with one," Papa said.

"Anyone threaten you, you fire first!"

"But what about Josiane?"

"One more reason to be with them," I said. "I help the Purifiers, maybe they'll bribe the cops to look for her."

11

GOD'S ARTILLERY

DEMON KILLER, in his most ornate uniform, was lecturing his troops from the big wooden platform. Behind Killer, Mpasi, and me was a huge TV screen the Purifiers had liberated from a shop in Kinshasa—we would use it to help teach the troops to fly reconnaissance drones. Bomb-capable drones could come later. Demon Killer was impatient to get started *now*, even if we'd been able to buy just a few little drones in Kinshasa for reconnaissance.

"Behold," Demon Killer said, holding a drone with a camera hanging from its bottom. "This is God's Little Airplane." He tossed the drone into the air while I fiddled with a tablet computer and guided the Little Airplane above the crowd.

"With this," he said, "our eyes are everywhere. God's Little Airplanes have cameras!" Via the aerial camera and the screen near us, the troops got a bird's eye view of themselves. "Look, you can see yourself on TV." The monitor showed what I was seeing on my Android tablet computer, aka a Little TV.

"No one will be safe from God's artillery," Demon Killer

said. "We'll show them on Little TVs and destroy them! No more Kias. No more government soldiers." The Purifier troops cheered. I brought the drones in for a safe landing on the platform, and Demon Killer beamed.

"Someday," he said, "our Little Airplanes will drop bombs! Because God loves us more and more each day!" Demon Killer pointed to Mpasi and me. "God handed down the word. Lemba first. Then Lemba taught Mpasi. They know their Little Airplanes and their Little TVs. They know how to use them to get money."

He grabbed my tablet computer and held it up for all the soldiers to see. "The banks, the big companies, the rich, everyone with money...no one is safe from us and our Little TVs. More money for you. More money to pay off the crooks of Kinshasa before we kill them. More money to buy more weapons and get all the oil and diamonds God wants us to have! More guns, too. The more guns we get, the holier we become."

A LARGE SOLAR cell array and small satellite dish, ordered from DarkMarket, sat outside our drone hut. Mick Jagger's music poured out of the loudspeaker of Mpasi's tablet, while little fingers snapped in time to the YouTube video.

"Come on, Mpasi," I said inside the hut, "have a heart...a little rumba, please. And turn it down, please."

Mpasi switched to a rumba Internet station.

"*Merci,*" I said. "Now, a little detail. Just how much do you really know about computers and drones?"

"Not much," Mpasi admitted, "but I can learn."

"But Demon Killer says you already know. Look! Here's a YouTube you should watch."

"Et maintenant, une introduction sur la cybersécurité," the announcer said. I paused the video. "Just what you need. How to protect yourself from viruses, phishing schemes, hacking, and so on."

Mpasi looked puzzled.

"Don't let the language scare you, Mpasi. It's all explained."

"I know I can do it," Mpasi said, "but you could also show me."

I nodded encouragingly. "Just remember," I said, "we'll be the ones making the attacks. We're the 'bad guys'!"

"When will we do the drones?"

"Now." We stepped outside, and I handed Mpasi the tablet computer used to control the drone that Demon Killer had boasted about earlier. Mpasi scrutinized it.

"Go ahead. Toss it into the air, like I showed you."

Mpasi did. The drone zig-zagged crazily above the camp, barely missing trees, as the others looked up alarmed.

None other than Demon Killer rushed over. "Lemba! Mpasi! What's going on?"

"Well, it's a new kind of drone for Mpasi. That's all."

The drone was descending a lot faster than I'd have wanted—and headed right toward Mpasi and me.

"Gently, Mpasi," I said. "Away from us."

Mpasi did just the reverse.

"It's OK, Mpasi," Demon Killer said as I ducked to avoid being hit. "God and Lemba will guide you not to kill us."

ONE DAY I discovered I couldn't get into bank computers as easily as before. Better security?

"But I thought your Little TVs would make us rich,"

Demon Killer said in the command hut as Mpasi and I briefed him. "Try, Lemba, try!"

"Something else," I said. "Someone has just stolen from us."

"Stolen?" Demon Killer roared. "Who? Tell me where they live—I will slay them in the name of God!"

"With DarkMarket," I said, "you can't always know who you're in touch with."

"I knew they were Satanic, with a name like that."

"But some good news," I said. "They didn't steal everything. We've still got plenty of money left."

"We can still buy more Little Airplanes?"

I nodded. "Yes, the money's there."

"And they can drop bombs?" he asked.

"Small ones," I said.

"Death to the Kias! Buy more airplanes!"

Mpasi's skills as a remote pilot finally improved. "Nice going," I said as he maneuvered the drone within several meters of the treetops at times. "I'll make a drone hacker out of you yet." I should have considered the ultimate consequences. But I was fixated on the challenges of the moment, and I enjoyed the aerial views of the lush jungle scenery.

Back at the base, Demon Killer told us, "Tomorrow, the Kias go to hell. Is your Little Airplane ready?"

So the next day I was flying our drone and seeing, below it, not just trees but humans—soldiers of the Kinshasa government. Demon Killer looked over my shoulder at the tablet screen. "What a sight!" he said. "Twenty devils awaiting their deaths!" He shared the view with a nearby artillery man. "God's eyes. We can see everything." The Purifiers started firing shell after shell at the Kias, and inspecting their remains a short time later, Demon Killer exalted, "God listened! We'll conquer them all. Soon bombs, not just TV!"

"But I'm still looking for the right drones."

"Hurry up," Demon Killer said. "If you care about your parents, then do what I say." Once again, I thanked God and fate that Killer hadn't mentioned Josiane.

In no time at all, Mpasi and I were watching a jut-jawed military man with a gravelly voice do a video pitch on Dark-Market, in English but with short captions in Arabic and French. How thoughtful. Upbeat music played in the commercial, videographed amid hills in an unnamed tropical county, as we watched the Eradicator drone in action. It could switch between an airplane-style fixed wing and a helicopter-style mode that allowed it to hover and go up and down.

The camera zoomed in to show small bombs attached to its underbelly. "With our jam-resistant technology," said Jut Jaw, "we can deliver military payloads of up to 35 pounds." Now the Eradicator swooped in over a cluster of soldiers, released a timed grenade-bomb and climbed up to safety. Flash! No more soldiers. Just corpses. It was as simple and scary as that. "The enemy...zapped! Just like a video game, except this is tactical air supremacy in real life."

Excited, tablet in hand, we rushed to show the commercial to Demon Killer. "That's it! God's Little Airplanes! God's bombs!"

"How many would you like us to buy?" Mpasi eagerly asked.

"There's just two of you," Demon Killer said.

"But don't you want us to teach others to fly them?" I asked.

Demon Killer smiled. "Of course! Imagine, a whole fleet of God's Little Airplanes! Truly we are blessed."

"Just to warn you," I said. "The government watches the ports and airports very carefully."

"May God strike them blind!"

Demon Killer thought he could bribe away the problem. But he soon found it wouldn't work, not when a very short-lived anti-corruption campaign was going on for PR purposes.

"DarkMarket won't even ship here," I said. "It isn't just the drones. The bombs, too. How can we get them in?"

"Remember," Demon Killer said, "I'm an old fisherman. The best kind of smuggler."

12

―――――

"I WILL KILL THE BABIES
BEFORE THEY KILL ME"

I WATCHED cranes from a dimly lit cargo ship loading up crates—with Eradicator drones and bombs—onto a fishing boat next to it. Demon Killer, Mpasi, and I were in the village of Yamwende on the Congo's tiny Atlantic Coast after our trip by boat and truck.

Franck Vangu, the owner of the fishing boat, was a slightly built man in sporty khakis who called his vessel *The Francine*. In his thirties, Vangu was apparently an old friend of Demon Killer. Vangu moved on deck with the confidence and energy of a go-getter and directed his helmsman the same way.

"You know," Vangu said, "I could use a few drones myself. Well, some friends of mine, pirates. Hijackings, robberies, that kind of thing."

"How's that, Franck?" Demon Killer asked.

"You be a pirate, you can always use a little more boom-boom," Vangu said.

"A pirate," said Mpasi, "now that I could be. Search for places to hide buried treasure. Why, it's just like hacking."

"You mean a guy who robs ships," I said. "Like the bad guys in the movies."

"But can't pirates be good?" Mpasi asked. "What's a few hijackings? The foreigners steal our oil, we make up for it."

After we returned to the Purifier camp, Demon Killer assembled his troops and held up the small drone that his forces had used earlier for reconnaissance against the Kias.

"God's Little Airplane," he said. "Did we not kill the Kias with our eyes in the sky?"

"Yes, Mon Général!" the soldiers replied.

Demon Killer gestured toward the heavens, then pointed to several blue drones on the platform. "And now... bigger Little Airplanes...to drop bombs...not just look down from above! How blessed we are!"

Mpasi and I would go on to preside over drone training sessions with 50 attendees while Demon Killer eagerly watched. An Eradicator Drone sat nearby.

"Anyone who does not know how to read," I said, "please leave."

Half the Purifiers in front of me did. It wasn't just a question of being able to read instructions. I wanted to work with the more intelligent people. Of course, a third of the 60 Purifiers there were children, many too young to read well, but others were grown adults—living examples of the illiteracy that had impoverished so many Congolese and helped thrust them into eternal wars with each other. I pitied them and felt more than a little elitist with my literacy requirement. But if I wanted my parents to live, then I must keep Demon Killer happy; and back in Zange, a bungled drone war might mean some fatal chops of Bota's machete.

"I'll show you everything," I said to my remaining volunteers. "For now, a test flight. Later, I make the final choices."

Via video games, I could help gauge their hand-eye coordination as well as their learning speed. But first the flight. The Eradicator rose straight up like a helicopter, then flew straight like a normal airplane, just as the commercial had promised.

"Behold," said "Demon Killer, "God's will on Earth! An enemy in view is an enemy ready to be bombed! And now we have the bombs!"

"Actually, Mon Général," I said, "it's a little more complicated than that."

"Lemba! Don't confuse them! They push the button when they hear the voice of God. It's that simple."

Mpasi and I once again were on the drill field, kicking an improvised football. I silently chided myself—I should have asked Demon Killer for a real one, as a perk of my new job as drone guru.

"My score," said Mpasi.

"If my gun says so," I said.

"Are you making fun of Demon Killer?" asked Mpasi.

"They push the button when they hear the voice of God," I mocked.

Mpasi angrily kicked the ball, and it was then that I *knew*: he was succumbing to the Purifiers' craziness. I was fighting at his side, but only to protect my parents, whom Demon Killer would have killed if I didn't cooperate.

"Please," I told Mpasi, "this isn't a video game. We'll be bombing real people. Helps to know if they're the right ones."

The next month, we were in the field for real—girding to attack the fortifications of government soldiers whom we knew to be several miles away, thanks to some well-targeted bribes. The aerial view would be good without thick foliage to hide the intruders. "It is time," Demon Killer said, "for them to feel the full wrath of God. Launch your airplanes."

Soldiers tapped on their tablets, and twenty Eradicator drones rose straight up and winged their way toward the government fortifications. We guided them on maps, then switched to the cameras, which showed far more Kias than we'd expected. "I can see them," Demon Killer rejoiced. "To see is to bomb. Everyone—listen to God's voice!" Our drones swooped in, ready to drop a mix of conventional and small incendiary bombs.

Pandemonium broke out after Mpasi, I, and the others gave our screens a few more taps. Flames devoured the Kias, turning them into ashes. What horrific deaths. I could see the killings in detail with my own eyes. The Purifiers had ordered us to bring the drones low for close-up videos and photographs to put up on the Web for propaganda purposes. Still, this was a world apart from killing enemies in the field and later being able to touch faces bearing expressions frozen in death.

I felt somewhat as if in a video game, or maybe simply playing one. I hated myself for doing so. I prayed for compassion to keep my humanity.

Most of our victims would not even undergo burials either because they would be missing or their bodies were in too many pieces. Dust to dust, in a sense. But that was God's role, not ours. I once again pondered all the widows we were creating, and all the sons and daughters without fathers to hug them or take them fishing or encourage them in football or school. Would a 15-year-old have thought like that? Not many, I'll grant you. But I did. That was my curse as a soldier and my salvation as a human, even if I still was not fully evolved.

I was flinching as Mpasi turned away from his tablet, perhaps to see how I was holding up. "You're worrying like a woman. Honor your gun! Honor God's Little Airplanes."

"'God's Little Airplanes'?" I asked. "They're only drones, nothing more."

"Well, that's the way Demon Killer says it. Do you really want to lick the Kias' boots? After what they did to Tiny's niece?"

The next day, Demon Killer carved additional marks into his forehead in honor of the new killings. It didn't matter that others had piloted the drones. He would take credit in the way most meaningful to him.

ALL THE CARNAGE from the heavens set me thinking. I was not yet so aware of the medical potential of drones, but I couldn't help wondering if they could be used to save lives, not end them.

Then I started mulling over my immediate circumstances—fantasizing, actually.

Suppose protective drones could hover above the heads of the people I loved. Guardian angels, so to speak—able to drop bombs on anybody even thinking of threatening my family. I prayed that Bota was truly protecting Mama and Papa. But guardian drones would still help.

What I needed, now, beyond that, was a drone which could magically find Josiane in a sprawling city of more than 17 million people.

My pain over my sister's disappearance only grew when I saw a new captive solider who reminded me so much of Josiane—everything from the high cheekbones to her height and long, confident strides. Perhaps we could be friends or more. But all hope faded when the lookalike volunteered as a drone operator and matched Mpasi's new passion for war crimes. As if that weren't enough, Demon Killer made Josiane's Evil Twin part of the personal harem he played with from time to time.

No, Demon Killer was not sullying my sister herself. The Evil Twin might even have been flattered. Still, I was repulsed by the thought of Demon Killer sleeping with someone who even just *looked* like Josiane.

THE RADIO BROUGHT us exciting news. A new diamond rush was on, in a location of the Congo far west of the previous discoveries.

"God's blessings," Demon Killer told Mpasi and me. "Lushitus is just a day from us."

"But we're soldiers, not miners," I said.

"Lemba! Who do you want the miners to dig up the diamonds for? Us, or the government? More Little Airplanes —that's what we need. With more airplanes, we can capture more diamonds!"

And so we went back to the little fishing town on the Atlantic Coast and picked up our next shipment of Eradicator drones.

"Just remember," said Vangu, just before our return to our base camp, "my friends are still interested. The freighters await us, ripe for the pickings!"

"Piracy?" Demon Killer protested. "That's small time."

"Just think of all these wars going on," Vangu said. "Lots of places to hold freighters for ransom!"

"But we have such a small coast."

"Who says it must be here?" Vangu asked. "Nigeria,

Angola, Gabon, Somalia—I've got friends, and friends of friends, all over the place. We could even do a tanker."

Demon Killer shook his head. "Who needs piracy? Who needs friends? I've got diamonds."

"Not yet," Vangu said. "Only if you succeed."

WITH THE ERADICATOR drones by his side, Demon Killer was strutting and haranguing once again on his wooden platform.

"God has spoken!" he told the troops. "The diamonds in time. But first we will cut off the head of the Kia beast. We know where their new regional headquarters are."

Demon Killer pointed to the Eradicators. "And now, enough Little Airplanes to finish the job! No Kias protecting the Kinshasa crooks' diamonds!" Bypassing me, Mpasi had gone behind my back and assured Demon Killer that this was a positive identification.

Just before the raid, I finally caught up with images of the proposed bombing site, downloaded freshly from the Eradicators. Instead of a military base, I saw a missionary hospital not that far from us. Why hadn't Demon Killer come to me rather than letting Mpasi tell him what he so badly wanted to hear? Angrily tapping my tablet screen, I told Mpasi, "I don't get it. How could *this* be a major Kia headquarters?"

"But all the soldiers, all the military vehicles, all the—"

"Yes," I said, "bringing in the wounded...military *patients*. It's a *hospital!*"

"Prove it," Mpasi challenged me.

"Do you see any weapons anywhere? Just medical people and patients."

"All I see is Kias in uniforms," Mpasi said.

I pointed to big red letters on a sign, next to a cross. "There! Read! St. Galois Missionary Hospital."

On top of everything else, the hospital was at least 50 kilometers from the diamond fields the Kia tribespeople were supposed to help the government protect. But Mpasi couldn't have cared less.

Walking over to Demon Killer's command hut, I contemplated how to undo the plans to pulverize the nonbase. Perhaps I could outdo Mpasi in appealing to the commandant's vanity.

No luck. Demon Killer was not the least apologetic, and, along the way, I learned he was actually doubling down on the plans for St. Galois. "Praise God, praise Mpasi," he said. "You are so fortunate to have such a divinely gifted assistant." I could tell by Demon Killer's face that he wasn't lying. He'd bought the fantasy to the max.

"And that's not all," I said, trying to steer him to a more benign one. "Now a vision has come to me."

"I told you God would speak to you!" Demon Killer said. "You and Mpasi, you're God's Little Airplane Children."

I nodded. "God is telling me we should not fly Little Airplanes today against the Kias. We must save our spiritual selves for greater things."

"What could be holier than diamonds for all of us?"

"Diamonds *and* power," I said. "We take over Kinshasa for sure, but we obey God right now!"

"But Mpasi says God's already spoken to him," Demon Killer said.

"What if it's a missionary hospital rather than a Kia headquarters?"

"Are you doubting God's word?" Demon Killer asked.

And then he called in Mpasi and said, "There's a change of plans."

"But I thought God agreed with our guns," Mpasi said. "We need to bomb the Kias for sure."

"No question!" Demon Killer said. "That's why I've called you in. I want you to begin the bombing now."

I wasn't on the scene when the drones attacked St. Galois, but later on, by way of an Internet TV station, I learned the details of the horrors. The hospital roof fell in flames. Medical people in white ran in all directions trying to rescue wounded patients, and some doctors and nurses and aides became victims themselves when the roof collapsed on them as well. More than 20 babies in the St. Galois maternity ward died along with their mothers.

Some of the Purifiers caught wind of what had happened. Most didn't care. But enough did to require another session of godly assurance from the wooden platform. "The radio says we're criminals," Demon Killer told the troops. "Are we criminals?"

"No!" the Purifiers roared back.

"Of course some children died," Demon Killer said. "Does God cry? No, because it was part of His plan. These Kias, they would have grown up to murder us! Say it! 'I will kill the babies before they kill me.'"

Suddenly artillery shells started landing near the Purifier camp. The Purifiers repelled the invaders, and that night Demon Killer vowed to retaliate with Little Airplane raids next time the government troops came near. He kept his word. Once again, transmissions from the Eradicators showed human-like images disappearing in clouds of flames.

"Will the demons ever learn?" Demon Killer told Mpasi. "Move in closer."

Mpasi obliged with his tablet.

"Yes," said Demon Killer, pointing at the screen, "kill those ones, too!" Mpasi did.

Smiling, Demon Killer congratulated him on his good work. "You have truly honored your gun."

13

FRANCINE THE BUTT-KICKER

A WHITE HELICOPTER bearing the UN insignia roared overhead. It lingered over the Purifier camp, then left without firing.

"That helicopter gives me bad feelings," I told Demon Killer. "And remember, they've got their own drones." Kinshasa also had been using drones at times. But up to now, at least, they hadn't gotten too far. I'd figured out how to jam them. I might not be able to do the same with the UN drones.

Luckily for Demon Killer, many of the blue-helmeted UN "peacekeepers" were far less scary than unjammable drones. Some even sold guns to his people. As with the government forces, the Purifiers often bribed them to stay out of the way while Demon Killer and friends raped, stole, and murdered. The purity suggested by the whiteness of the helicopter was grotesquely misleading, especially since certain of the "peacekeepers" also had assaulted and impregnated Congolese women. Of course, in my ideal world, black would be just as holy.

Demon Killer mulled over the coming of the helicopter,

pulled out a pistol, and stroked its barrel for divine insights. "Yes, God's sign," he finally said regardless of the copter's Satanic connections. "We need to move on." He told me the Kinshasa crooks at the moment were outbidding his bagmen.

"Where to?" I asked.

Demon Killer stroked his pistol some more, and then he shared what God had told him through it.

"You'll be pirates for real," he said happily to Mpasi and me.

"But you said it didn't pay enough."

"God has corrected me. Go out to sea with His Little Airplanes, and all the other pirates will be jealous."

"More boom-boom!" Mpasi said.

I toyed again with the notion of growing rich from humoring Demon Killer and then bribing the right officials to find Josiane. But on second thought, would I really get my money's worth? The Kinshasa crooks might just take the cash and do nothing.

"I don't need to be rich," I told Demon Killer.

"But you need your parents, right? Better that Bota chop crops. Better than their heads, no?"

And so I left with Demon Killer and a band of other Purifiers to the coastal fishing village from which we would venture forth to hijack ships.

Traveling back to Yamwende by truck and boat, we broke up into small groups and used cellphones as infrequently as possible. I also disabled the phones' tracking mechanisms and took other precautions to try to keep us off the minds of the Kinshasa thieves.

Demon Killer's fixers worked their own magic during the evacuation. Once again, despite the new uncertainty, a little bribery of the right people helped.

WHEN VANGU GREETED us in his hilltop home in Yamwende, we saw a curvy light-skinned young woman in her twenties by his side. She wore tight-fitting khakis and a diamond ring and spoke in a surprisingly educated voice.

"Who's your lady friend?" Demon Killer asked Vangu.

"This is Francine, and she can kick butt."

"Not mine," Demon Killer said.

The two men laughed.

"We'll see about that," Vangu said. "You should see her in action with her AK!"

Demon Killer was staring now at Francine's breasts. "I like her boom-booms."

"Property of Vangu," responded the object of Demon Killer's attention.

"Forgive my uncle," Vangu said to Francine. Clearly, he was flustered.

"Is he really your uncle?" I asked Vangu.

"Tell him!" Vangu said to Demon Killer. "It's time. No use to hide anymore."

"But I am still your Général of all Générals," Demon Killer told Mpasi and me.

"Mon Général of *all* Générals," I said, nodding as energetically as possible, "I could think of you as nothing else."

"Me, too," Mpasi said.

Led by Vangu, we walked to an eatery lower on the hill and, with rumba music playing, ordered fish and rice. The music drowned out our conversion. Later, when we got down to business, we could talk freely.

Vangu fondly looked at Francine. "She's my girl. Why, I even renamed my boat after her."

"How'd you meet her?" Demon Killer asked.

"Fate and computer dating," Vangu said. "Shared love of adventure. A perfect match!"

"What? I don't understand."

"Just understand," said Vangu, "that she can whip your ass."

"A woman?" responded Demon Killer.

Francine set her arm on the table for an arm-wrestling match.

"See for yourself," Vangu said.

Demon Killer extended his arm. "Don't worry," he said to Francine. "I'll be gentle."

It was no contest—Francine won.

"I work out," Francine said, "just in case." She winked.

"You're just lucky catching me on a bad day," Demon Killer said.

Everyone laughed, with one obvious exception.

"You got a sister?" Demon Killer asked Francine.

"Careful what you wish for," said Francine, smiling. "You think *I'm* tough?"

I waited for Demon Killer to find out more about the sister. But for now, I thought, he didn't want to face another possible humiliation.

"Where you from?" he asked her.

"All over the place," Francine said.

"Francine and I," Vangu said, "we do a lot of traveling."

She was actually from Cabinda, Angola, where the educated spoke French. She had even studied in Paris, the birthplace of her white father, the wayward scion of a rich Parisian family.

I enjoyed the way Francine talked. I wondered if, magically, my French could be as good someday as hers. Josiane's own French, at least, was better than mine.

Francine turned to me. "Lemba," she said, "I hear you're a computer genius."

"Think drones," Vangu said to me. "Think ships."

"Think pirate, think ransom money," Francine said. "That's what it's all about."

Demon Killer shot a fierce look at me, and, on cue, I nodded.

"And plenty else," Vangu said. "All that oil stolen. All the greedy politicians and their foreign friends."

He and his uncle, as crooks and thieves, were proud of their level of political consciousness. All the better to rationalize their crimes.

"It's God's will," Demon Killer said. "We're going to take it all back."

"We could collect the ransoms in CryptoGhosts," I said.

"CryptoGhosts?"

"A way to move money from one computer to the next. No one knows who you are if you do it right." CryptoGhosts were a more secure form of digital currency than the old bitcoins.

"What's the range of your drones?" Francine asked me.

"Depends on their size and the bomb load. Maybe 15 kilometers."

"Excellent," said Francine as crisply as ever. "We can launch them from our boats and spy on ships."

"I've got two of the newer models," I said, "extra quiet and black. Almost invisible at night."

"Didn't I tell you?" Vangu exulted to Demon Killer. "Knowledge is holiness." I doubted Vangu was that religious —but he knew what his uncle wanted to hear.

"But," I asked, "what if there's a better way?"

And there was.

MPASI and I set up a satellite dish and solar cells in a large hut near Vangu's house as Demon Killer, his nephew, and Francine watched admiringly. Then with a tablet and a laptop, we called up a global maritime map with tiny red, green, and blue dots.

"These are ships moving north along the West African Coast," I said.

I clicked on a dot and both screens filled with the photo of a container cargo ship named *The Sea Mule*. More clicks revealed it was headed toward the Democratic Republic of the Congo's teeny Atlantic coast.

"That's it," I said excitedly. "The one we might go after! Just a few days away from us."

I tapped on a link. An electronic manifest listing appeared in English showing what *The Sea Mule* was carrying.

"Look," I said, "TVs, cellphones, automobiles—"

"I want!" said Demon Killer

With a few more taps, I found a screen indicating the total value. 230 million euros.

"DarkMarket would make it so simple for me," I said.

"To do what?" Vangu asked.

"Tell the ship where to go," I said. "They got all kinds of crazy stuff to crack with. Just a few quick downloads." Something caught my eye. *"Mon Dieu!"* The database said *The Sea Mule* would soon be visiting Kongo Central, the province encompassing the small coastline.

"Maybe," I said, "we can intercept it before it stops in Boma. What if we could change its speed and route a little?" I started typing furiously away on my laptop.

When the sun set, I was still tapping away.

14

UNCLE OSCAR'S AMAZON

Francine brought me a breakfast of crunchy fried fish. Mpasi was still asleep.

"Look," I said, yawning, "a different route now! I'm in the shipper's database!" A map now showed a slightly different route for *The Sea Mule*. The database bore the logo "Melton Shipping."

Francine laughed and clapped. I enjoyed her encouragement. It reminded me a little of Josiane's own cheerleading for me. "You should work for a shipping company," Francine said. "Imagine—the ship coming to us! Go, Lemba!"

"Here's a map of the ship and cargo." I flipped through different screens showing the floor plans of each level. We saw the engine room.

"Let's see if it has 'Search by name,'" Francine said.

I clicked to bring up the appropriate search screen.

"Excellent," said Francine in her most encouraging maternal voice. "Now look for something called a safe room."

I keyed in those words. A digital map of the ship zeroed in the safe room, complete with that description.

"So that's where they'll hide," Francine said. "'Play turtle.' Old story. We'll just crack the shell."

I told *The Sea Mule* to slow down by three knots, and it immediately obliged. I remembered the huge, hulking ship in the photo, full of thousands of tons of container cargo. Imagine me, Lemba, just 15, bossing all that machinery.

For good measure, having quickly hacked the format and language of shore-to-ship email, I sent a message to the crew confirming that the changes were legitimate. No one challenged me.

"What about security guards?" Vangu asked.

"No information on that."

"But who says there won't be blood?" Demon Killer said as if eagerly anticipating it. "No one messes with the Général of all Générals!"

"Or Vangu," his nephew said. "We threaten the crew. Plant explosives. Maybe even sink the ship if they don't pay. But only if! They pay, nothing more happens."

"But what becomes of us?" Demon Killer asked.

"We just get to the lifeboat first," Vangu said, "And then our Angolan friends take us away. Big, fast motorboat."

"But Monsieur," I asked, wondering who these friends happened to be, "what if your fishing boat gets blown up along with the ship?"

"Who gives a crap? The ransom money—we could buy hundreds of boats."

"Uncle Oscar," said Francine to Demon Killer, "I've got a surprise for you."

"Oh?"

"You asked to meet my sister," she said.

"And she has boom-booms just like yours?"

"Bigger," said Francine, "and she'll be helping us out on the raid."

"Wow, wow!" Demon Killer said. "I can't wait!"

AT A BEACH NEAR YAMWENDE, we reviewed our collection of armaments. I could see piles of AK-47s, RPGs, and other armaments—enough explosives to sink even a giant container ship, or at least put a good-sized dent in it. The night came, and everyone just sat around a fire drinking palm wine. Of course, the day of the hijacking, kola nuts would be more like it. We'd chew on the nuts and be a little more alert from the caffeine in them.

"You're sure you can do it, Lemba?" Vangu asked.

How could anything go wrong? The ship always responded when I gave it instructions. There'd be no chase. And we could enjoy the cover of darkness. Not much worry about radar, either. The blips would suggest just a small fishing boat and so on. No need for a chase. We'd guide our target to us.

Once aboard, we'd know exactly where to go to wire up the most valuable cargo to explode if the crew defied us. For good measure, we could even threaten to sink the whole ship—and do it.

"But how do we trigger the explosives?" Demon Killer asked.

"Here's our new toy," said Vangu, and held up a small cellphone-like slab from his pocket. The slab contained a series of buttons and a screen like the one on a cellphone.

"It's fool-proof," I told Demon Killer. "You just tap out a code for stuff you want to blow up."

"Three taps on the green button means the whole ship," Vangu said, "or at least the bridge area."

"You wouldn't really do it, would you?" Francine asked.

"Of course not," Vangu said. "But I still find strength in it. Every day I can look at the green button and know I'll never back down."

"Who's going to cook?" Demon Killer asked. "They be stubborn, we could be at it for days."

"Who cares?" Vangu said.

"What if they poison us? Maybe bring our own rations."

"Relax, Uncle Oscar," Francine said. "Not everyone's like you. No need to hate everyone."

Vangu nodded. "No hate, no religion, no prayer, just business. I'll die for only one cause."

"Which one, Monsieur?" I asked.

"Myself."

"NEXT BOAT?" Demon Killer asked eagerly as we looked over the water, awaiting the arrival of Francine's sister.

"I'm sure of it," Francine said.

"Look!" I said. "Over there." A boat was approaching.

"Maybe that's the one," she said.

The boat docked, and Francine smiled and waved to a tall, big-bosomed woman of about 25, nearly Demon Killer's height, with a broad body. Francine rushed forward to hug her as the passenger stepped onto the wharf. The Amazon was making child's play out of carrying a gigantic knapsack along with her much-lighter AK-47.

"Oh Monique," Francine said, "how I've missed you!"

"This must be the mighty warrior you were telling me about," Monique said, smiling at Demon Killer.

Monique reached out an oversized hand. Reluctantly, Demon Killer shook it.

"She doesn't look like you," Demon Killer said to Francine.

"You wanted big boom-booms." Monique's, in fact, were huge, like everything else on her. "Actually she's my *half-sister*. But close enough."

Monique turned to Demon Killer. "Mon Cher, we'll make a great team!"

Demon Killer appeared to grimace.

"Oh, come on," Francine said. "You'll be glad Monique's with us. You think *I'm* good with an AK?"

"Ship still on time?" Vangu asked me.

"Just a day or so away."

Inspired by Francine and Monique, we did push-ups to stay in shape, in between oiling our AK-47s and other chores. Then Demon Killer, egotistical as ever, challenged Monique to an arm-wrestling match. He'd already lost to Francine, half her size, but megalomania and narcissism do not always result in the best judgment.

No, I need not tell you the winner. Undaunted, Demon Killer then requested a full wrestling match, but both women scoffed at the notion, lest Monique accidentally break some bones. His. In a way I was surprised Demon Killer was even still on speaking terms with the two sisters. He normally was not the best of losers.

15

———

GREEDSTER DREAMS

VANGU and I were watching soldiers load the AK-47s, detonators, explosives, and other weapons aboard his fishing boat, along with a portable cutting torch and a rope ladder. We also fiddled with one of the master detonators. Then we made small-talk about Nigerian action movies—Francine had even acted in one as an extra—and video games.

In character for his family, Vangu boastfully challenged me to play a Chinese action-adventure game with him after we returned from the hijacking. He'd better be careful, so I wouldn't do to him on the screen what Monique had done to Demon Killer in the hand-wrestling match. But why bring on trouble? I swore I'd control myself and lose.

Then, out of nowhere, Vangu put me in a game in real life—this kind of suspense I didn't need.

"I know about you and my uncle," Vangu said. "'Just like a chicken.'" Vangu clucked and imitated his uncle's throat-slitting noise.

"Monsieur," I said, "that's between Demon Killer and me."

"He even brags about it. I'd say you could use a friend. Your parents, too. Notably me."

"I'd say Demon Killer's protection is enough."

"If you can trust him. A man like that, you want him to keep so much of the ransom? What if you and I do a few tricks with those CryptoGhosts? You know, just to make sure we get our share." Poor Vangu. He'd been around greedsters so long that he thought I might be the same way.

"Excuse me, Monsieur," I said, "but I'd like to double-check that detonator."

"He'll never miss what he didn't know he had. In fact, who says he has to be around to collect any ransom at all?"

"Monsieur, please. I need to focus on my work."

That included staying alive.

VANGU REMAINED AT THE WHARF, but I returned to his house to fire up the laptop, check up on the whereabouts of *The Sea Mule*, and plan accordingly. That was the excuse I'd concocted, anyway.

In the garden I caught up with Demon Killer, who had been in the middle of a gun worship ritual. I let him chant for a while as he lovingly cleaned his weapon, running a snakelike device through the barrel from the chamber a few times. He used a wire brush on the other parts. Demon Killer did this again and again—an obsessive-compulsive in the service of his god.

He didn't notice me at all. He was too engrossed in his cleaning ritual. What was the Purification Army without its leader firing off the very most purified gun? How he cherished his AK!

Demon Killer, however, had suddenly also grown super-affectionate toward a fellow gun-lover—Monique. I chanced across him sneaking in a quick tryst in the bushes toward a far corner of Vangu's big lot.

Chemically and in other ways, they'd become an instant couple. I was surprised. Who'd have imagined that Demon Killer's passion for Monique's boom-booms and the rest of her almost equaled his feelings for AK-47s? His faked indifference toward her must have been just a bargaining chip. She had turned out to be his type after all —well, within bounds. Demon Killer's real "type" fired bullets.

Demon Killer performed his sacred cleaning ceremony solo, without even Monique around. He would work on his AK in public at times, but without his chants, unintelligible and punctuated by a few animalistic grunts, this wasn't a full-fledged ritual.

"Mon Général of All Générals," I finally said, "would you give my parents yet another hand in the fields if I did you a favor?" Perhaps I shouldn't have said that. But Mama and Papa were already on his radar, and besides, in breaking the news about Franck Vangu, I would be gaining more leverage.

Demon Killer looked up. "Not now. I'm almost done."

I returned 20 minutes later and again broached the question.

"Whatever my gun told me to do," Demon Killer said.

"But you would?"

"Isn't it enough of a favor to keep your parents alive?" Demon Killer said. "You cross me, you die too. Pray to your gun."

"But you'd keep your word if I saved your life?"

"Of course. No life is worthier than mine."

"Another field hand for my parents if you find I've

earned it," I said. "Someone also handy with a machete if the bad guys show up."

"Bota's not working out?"

"No, I mean a second one to help out."

"Yes," Demon Killer said. "Another big guy with a big machete."

"So now I need to keep my end of the bargain. Vangu wants to kill you."

Demon Killer laughed. "Is this a joke?"

"It's about the ransom money," I said.

"A greedy little thing, but still family. But let's pretend. Let's say you're right."

"I heard it with my own ears."

"We'll even have a contract. Everything's fine."

Demon Killer was in one of his dumber moments, of course. As if killer nephews honored contracts! I couldn't believe that Demon Killer actually loved Vangu enough to trust him that much.

He stroked his gun as if to receive wisdom from it.

"I kill him now," he said, "I still need a boat. Anyway, we're still talking it over. You know—who gets how much."

"So should I tell him I'll go along and—"

"Lemba, you think too much. Just listen to your gun and all will be fine."

"But the Angolans. We need them to—"

"Stop it! Our guns will help us escape. But that's jumping ahead."

"Jumping ahead?" I asked.

"Would my own nephew really...You pull any tricks on me, you're fish food." Ah! The standard threat. But breathing the salty air, there in a seaside village, made it scarier.

16
———

HIJACK DAY

Hɪᴊᴀᴄᴋ Dᴀʏ, as we called it, was finally here. The fishing boat pulled away from the wharf, towing two high-speed skiffs. Vangu was piloting with me nearby. The land receded over the horizon, and a few hours later, I was seeing *The Sea Mule*'s radar blips. "Look," I said, "right on time."

"We slow down here?" Vangu asked.

"Oui! We're on their path—well, close enough. Let them come to us."

Suddenly Demon Killer stormed into the cabin, followed by a worried-looking Monique.

"I thought we'd agreed!" he told Vangu. "70 percent for me, 30 for you. And now Monique tells me…"

"If only you could read better. Look." Vangu stopped *The Francine* and reached into his pocket for the contract they'd drawn up. He showed Demon Killer clause C in the French document. And off in the margin—a fish-style mark from the Mighty Warrior. "It's my boat," Vangu said, "and my contacts for the get-away."

"But most of the people come from me," Demon Killer

said. "I even got you our Little Airplane genius. The smarter we are, the more we can steal."

"60-40," said Vangu, "and you're to pay your people from your share."

"No, 70-30," Demon Killer said. "Here I thought I could trust you!"

"You changed the contract!" Monique said.

Vangu screamed his denial. "No Vangu, no boat, no hijacking, no ransom money."

Demon Killer looked at me, then back at Vangu. "Then it is true. Money over blood!"

Vangu feigned ignorance. Not a tremble.

Turning to me, Demon Killer said, "Tell Vangu what he told you."

"You wanted to cheat Demon Killer," I said.

"Just *cheat?*" Demon Killer said before Vangu could utter a syllable back. "Isn't there more?"

"You wanted to kill your own uncle," I told Vangu. Imagine growing up in a family like that, as opposed to one with the ever-nurturing Josiane and my gentle parents.

"Liar!" Vangu shouted.

"Impossible now," Demon Killer said, and lunged for Vangu. "Because," he said with his arms around Vangu's neck, "I'm going to kill you first."

Francine started to reach for her knife, but Monique was too quick. She began to strangle Francine before changing her mind and instead beating her sister to death. Demon Killer, meanwhile, had snapped Vangu's neck without further moves needed. He gazed down at the bodies, then asked me: "Want to help me feed the fishes?"

Demon Killer started dragging out Vangu's corpse to throw overboard but took a moment to point to Francine's remains. "Go ahead," Demon Killer said. "Help me take out the trash."

"I'm sorry about your sister," I told Monique.

"*Half*-sister," Monique said. "She just didn't understand." She looked fondly at Demon Killer. "A mighty warrior must have his way."

Demon Killer turned to me. "There is one thing you must teach me."

"Whatever you want, Mon Général."

"How to work that detonator box."

We arranged for a replacement at the helm. Then we returned to the business of tossing the bodies over the side, while the child soldiers looked on expressionless. I don't think Vangu and Francine's deaths had made that much of an impression on them. This was just a little mayhem atop the hangings and other executions they'd already witnessed back at the Purifiers' camp. Not to mention all the violence that the Purifiers had forced the young ones to commit themselves. I myself took the trauma rather stoically. Vangu had been a no-good scoundrel who, for all I knew, would have sold me out if I'd gone along with his scheme.

So despite my youth, I didn't weep a tear over the corpses. Vangu could easily have murdered Demon Killer, one way or another, rather than the other way around. I'd miss Francine more, even if my eyes stayed dry. I would forever remember the maternal encouragement she offered me, the budding pirate, as well as the French she spoke so precisely in her feminine, almost-musical voice.

After these latest killings, Demon Killer couldn't resist a chance to act concerned and reinforce his holy ways among the children. "An accident," he told them in his most reassuring tone. "This is what happens when you don't listen to your gun."

IT WAS DARK NOW—PERHAPS we should have said "Hijack Night" rather than "Hijack Day."

With our lights out, the fishing boat moved close to *The Sea Mule*. I hoped our ladder would be tall enough. At least from far off, there in the dim moonlight, it looked as if the deck might loom 10 meters above us.

"Ready?" I asked Mpasi, who nodded.

"Happy fish mongering," I said while chewing on kola nuts, and then we put out Mpasi in a dinghy, which he paddled.

I wasn't with Mpasi in the dinghy, but he later shared with me some of the craziness of his first encounter with *The Sea Mule* and the crew. Most pirates might simply have tried to sneak aboard in the cover of night. But against my advice, the late Vangu had decided to experiment with a distraction, and Demon Killer overruled me and stuck to the crazy plan. So in his dinghy Mpasi played loud music on a transistor radio and looked as if he were fishing, rod in hand. He floated with the waves parallel to the ship.

A guard peered over the rails. Mpasi couldn't tell if the man was carrying a machine gun, but ideally his story would cause the men to relax their vigilance, so this didn't matter anyway.

"Ahoy there!" said a guard, first in English, then French. "Away from the ship! You'll get swamped."

Mpasi swung a West African Croaker we'd given him. "Do you want fresh fish?"

A second guard pointed a strong flashlight beam at the dinghy. "Only one fish?" he asked in an amused way.

"I have two," Mpasi said. "Boy and girl. Four euros."

"What are you doing out here?"

"Fishing. You want the fish or not? You lower bucket with money, I give you fish."

Bizarrely enough, the men obliged him.

My theory is that the guards were as nutty as Vangu, Demon Killer, and Mpasi—or, more likely, just underpaid and stupid. *I'd* have lowered not the bucket but a boat instead to rescue the fool, assuming I didn't correctly guess it was a pirate's ploy. But against all logic, Mpasi not only distracted the guards, he made a sale.

"*C'est moi*," he said into a tiny walkie-talkie, out of sight of the guards. "Got 'em busy with the fish."

At that point I sent up a pair of quiet black reconnaissance drones with cameras able to help monitor *The Sea Mule* and its crew in dim light. Then we launched two skiffs with almost-silent trolling motors in case they needed more speed. Skiff #1 contained Demon Killer, Monique, me, and several Purifier kids. Skiff #2 carried a few more children and several adults. It was past 2 a.m. with the moon shining on the other side of *The Sea Mule*, and the skiffs slid quietly into a shadowed location by the big ship.

Monique and Demon Killer looked up and around—no crew members were visible on the deck above us. Nor did the drone transmissions, as viewed on my phone, show any nearby threats. Monique used long bamboo rods with hooks to get a grip on the ship, and the rope ladder followed. AK-47s strapped to their backs, Monique and Demon Killer were the first aboard. I still couldn't get over how the distraction was working. On top of everything else, we'd lucked out and boarded an area without any of the crew members around at the time.

The rest of us helped Monique and Demon Killer haul up buckets with more AK-47s and explosives. Once regrouped on the deck, we spread out as planned.

A loud alarm blared away, but helpfully the guards were still far off on the other side of the ship, and we figured we'd have a little more time before *The Sea Mule* started spraying defensive walls of water and fending us off in other ways. No such luck. Floodlights lit up the ship like a meteor, and a flare shot into the sky; amid the brightness, we now could truly say, "Hijack *Day*." Then the water walls went up.

But by this time, just about all of us were aboard and scattering around the ship.

I trailed Demon Killer and Monique, and a mix of other pirates, young and old, followed. We rushed up toward the superstructure housing the wheelhouse at the top. The closest security guards shot at us. We fired back. Monique's AK took care of much of the remaining resistance. Other pirates were busy elsewhere, rigging huge shipping containers with explosives. Finally a band of us reached the wheelhouse and aimed our AK-47s at three men I would later learn to be Captain Hank Chandler, Communications Officer Phil Kelly, and Steersman Fred O'Neill. I soon discovered that the comm officer was among the few non-whites really in control of the ship. Racism gone to sea? I had hoped *The Sea Mule* was an exception.

"On the floor, all of you!" Demon Killer cried. "Hands on head, in the name of God!" Here and at many other times during the hijacking, I translated, taking care to act out Demon Killer's full craziness.

The men obeyed.

"I'm Captain," said Capt. Chandler, cautiously looking up. "So how much?" He was a heavy-set man of middling height and had a big indentation in his forehead. From an operation, or a bashing with a heavy metal object during a fight?

"Oh, Captain," Monique said in English with a refined

French accent belying her rougher side, "aren't you a little ahead of yourself? Where's the rest of the crew?"

"Who knows?" he said. "It's a big ship."

"I know. Safe room. Just by the engines." The database, of course, had already revealed its location.

"Then why are you asking—"

"Liar!" Monique said. "That's what you're paid to say."

As she spoke, Purifiers started tying up the *Sea Mule* men in the wheelhouse.

"Find them all," Demon Killer said. "Every crew member for ransom. And no guns for infidels! Take 'em away."

A few Purifiers and I returned to *The Francine*, the late Vangu's fishing boat, and pulled it up alongside *The Sea Mule* near the rope ladder. We used a net to hoist aboard a cutting torch and fuel and oxygen tanks. They were heavy. But we still managed to haul them up and rush toward the safe room in the already-known location—except that it wasn't there. Just a locked but empty room.

"Lemba," said Monique, "how can I trust you? I thought we had the location nailed down."

"We're just following what the ship's plans said."

"How could you mess up like this?" she asked. "Are you trying to sabotage us?"

"When we've gotten this far?"

"But why wouldn't the plans be accurate? I've got some pretty bad vibes."

For a moment, I wondered if at some point I would be tangling with Monique. Francine hadn't fared too well. I was strong for my age, not a midget, but I still could not believe how I'd turned the tables on Tiny and Sako. This time I might not be so lucky. What should I do? Try to torch Monique if she made the first move?

But instead I torched open the door across the hall, which, mercifully, was the one for the safe room.

The blowtorch was powerful enough for the cutting to happen in no time at all. Through the hole we saw lights and heard noises. But I dared not peep inside but for a second, lest someone in fact find time to fire.

Entering the safe room, AK-47s ready, we watched the crew members put their hands up even before we said so. Maybe they'd been more conscientious about their training than the people in the wheelhouse.

"Against the wall!" Monique yelled, and the crew members obeyed.

We started tying them up. A security guard—as it turned out—reached down as if for a sidearm. But Monique was too quick with her AK, and, a big, bloody hole in his chest, he fell.

"Stupid man," Monique said to our captives. "You're safer with him dead."

17

"PIRATE CENTRAL" NEGOTIATES

ALL THE CREWMEN we'd found in the wheelhouse were tied up now, even the steersman. *The Sea Mule* sat dead in the water. No need for anyone to steer right now.

With Vangu turned into fish food, I'd be the negotiator. Demon Killer had actually recognized his limits, and even Monique shied away, figuring I would be more comfortable with large numbers. Besides, in their minds, I was only setting the stage for the final deal that the Mighty Warrior would sign off on. I wondered if he'd reserved a place on his face for a dot to signify *that*.

"Mon Capitaine," I told Captain Chandler, "we're prepared to blow up things if you don't pay. Cars. TVs. Computers. All 230 million euros of them."

Captain Chandler, white-haired, looked too frail for me to expect much of a fight from him despite his forehead indentation hinting of a violent event in his past.

But he glared at Demon Killer, and in a semi-growl said belligerently, "Pretty sad—bringing kids into this."

Monique laughed, smiled, and revealed with almost-motherly pride that I, Lemba, had told the ship to go to this location and slow down. Of course, the scope and level of the pride were somewhat limited.

"I'm the one," I rubbed it in.

"Well," said the communications officer, Phil Kelly, a small, scholarly-looking man who seemed out of place on the ship, "it also could have been me."

"Excuse me, Monsieur?"

"They almost kicked me out of the Maritime Academy," he said. "All the pranks I pulled on their computers."

"Lemba," Monique said, "ignore him! He's just trying to soften you up."

Captain Chandler kept staring at the marks on Demon Killer's forehead, and Killer picked up on that in a flash. "Enemies killed. Do you want to be a dot?"

"A little problem," the Captain said, calming down slightly. "Our sat phone and the rest aren't working."

Monique laughed and turned to me. "Nice going."

Captain Chandler looked puzzled.

"Your phones and everything else—all knocked out," she said. "Jammed."

"OK," Monique said to me, "get the Captain's phone and email back on."

I nodded, reached into my backpack for a tablet computer and started tapping away on the screen. Then I turned to Mon Capitaine and said, "A very reasonable ransom. Just 23 million euros."

By now the sun was dawning. I heard the squawks of a few seagulls flying overhead. The ship remained dead in the water. I was about to take a brief nap while Demon Killer, Monique, and Mpasi guarded the captives in the wheelhouse. But then the maritime phone buzzed, and I reached for it. I didn't have to guess who was at the other end—

someone from the shipping company. Almost surely, *The Sea Mule* had radioed news of the boarding.

How to answer? "Pirate Central"? Instead I simply said, "Lemba here."

"I need to talk to Captain Chandler," said a voice in American-accented English. I felt a trifle offended. Couldn't this man have shown a little respect and instead started out in French? Did he even know how to speak it?

"Perhaps, Monsieur," I said, "you need to talk to me instead." Maybe I should have said "sir" since I was speaking in the English I'd learned online, but the Francophone in me prevailed.

The man himself sounded sleepy. The East Coast of America was something like five time zones away.

"Who are you?" demanded the caller.

My voice was starting to deepen, and he actually did not ask my age. Luckily he could not see me. While I was already a good 1.85 meters tall, my face was still in transition from boyhood to manhood. My brown eyes were childishly large. In person I looked too young and friendly to do harm.

"Does it matter?" I said when the man pressed me further. "Here's what does. 23 million euros, and the ship and cargo are yours again."

"Unacceptable."

"And who," I asked, "are *you*?"

"Fred Montoya. Authorized negotiator for Melton Shipping." Some companies hired professional negotiators and dealt with pirates in a leisurely way. But Melton apparently was too cheap and too much in a hurry to get *The Sea Mule* back.

"Easy to pay," I said. "Just a tenth of the insured value of cargo. CryptoGhosts, please."

"Maybe 150,000 euros."

"Not enough, Monsieur," I said. "23 million euros is a bargain. You waste our time, we'll add the cost of the ship."

"The US Navy is now on your tail," said Monsieur Montoya.

"But Monsieur," I said, "we've got explosives all over the ship."

For the benefit of Captain Chandler, who was watching, Demon Killer pulled out the detonator from his pocket as I talked to Monsieur Montoya.

Demon Killer tapped on the device but avoided the green button. As promised, almost immediately after Vangu's killing, I'd taught him how to use the detonator. I just hoped that he would keep his buttons straight.

"Monsieur," I said to the shipping executive, "how would you like us to blow up the circuit boxes for the refrigerators? A nice start."

"I told you," said Monsieur Montoya, "150,000 euros."

"You've got 1.5 million euros of New Zealand lamb down there."

For some reason, Monique was licking her lips at the word "lamb." I wondered if she wanted some of the cargo.

"Maybe 175,000 euros," Monsieur Montoya said. "Nothing more."

"And then," I said, "we go on to the electronics. The Samsung TVs. The cellphones. The computers."

"Is the crew OK?" Monsieur Montoya asked.

"Very happy," I said. "I hear they've got a poker game going in the lock-up room. Yes, very happy. All locked up together except for the Captain and friends."

"200,000 euros," Monsieur Montoya said, "and that's it."

"23 million euros in two days, Monsieur," I said, "or you lose ship, crew, and cargo."

I hung up.

"Good job," said Demon Killer. "Right now we celebrate our victory." He turned to me. "You and Mpasi, you keep an eye on the prisoners."

I laughed inside—I myself was a captive of sorts. But, yes, I was a smart, realistic boy and just nodded. I preferred that Bota and his friend use their machetes only on *crops*.

"We can't celebrate without a feast," Monique said. "Lamb chops—I want lamb chops!"

AK-47s in hand, she and I went down to the galley with Communications Officer Kelly. He'd said he was a friend of the kitchen help, had watched them at work, and knew where the basics were.

"The cook would throw a fit, me doing this," Officer Kelly said as he removed beans from a cabinet. "Union rules." He picked up a big tin of rice. "We can do Angolan if you want."

Monique shook her head. "No—Congolese-style, *exactly*. What Demon Killer wants, Demon Killer gets. And lamb and cake for all! A Mighty Warrior must have his way!"

"OK, *Congolese* rice and beans," said Officer Kelly. A sensible choice, with Monique pointing her AK-47 at him. "Or I can do Cameroon. My grandfather's from there."

"I told you—Congolese," Monique said. "Never mind. I'll cook it myself." She handed the weapon to me. "You guard him."

Then, perhaps hoping Monique would be distracted or comfortable enough not to interfere, Officer Kelly asked me, "Do you read books? Goes with being a sailor. Lots of time at sea."

"No books," I said. "But technical stuff on my tablet. OK, maybe some Jules Verne."

"Well, here's a book to read when you're ready. *Heart of Darkness*."

"Maybe someday," I said.

"Maybe you can look it up in Wikipedia."

"It's that good a book?" I asked.

"Actually, it's a very bad book. Lots of lies about Africa by a mixed-up white man. But that's the point."

"Excuse me, Monsieur?"

"Well, there's some bad stuff in there from a guy named Kurtz: 'Exterminate all the brutes!' Lemba, we've got to do better! We must not be our own brutes."

"I try my best, Monsieur."

"I saw it on CNN," Officer Kelly said. "The hospital. The drone attack. Have anything to do with you guys? Directly or not?"

I didn't utter a syllable, but I'm certain Officer Kelly must have noticed my quiver.

"All right," he said, "I'm not going to pester you. But just remember, whatever the technology, don't be a techno-brute —use it for the good. Don't be a brute of any kind."

I guess that was his way of reprimanding me without pushing it too far, given that I was the one with the AK-47 dutifully aimed at him.

"No cake mix anywhere," Monique interrupted.

"But we're almost out of places to look," Officer Kelly said. "Maybe we need to get the cook." Laughing, he told me, "I guess you could say we're 'hacking' the kitchen."

I picked up the prompt. "Did you really mess with the computers at your school?"

"Once upon a time," Officer Kelly said, scouring the kitchen for the cake mix.

"You raised your grades?"

"If only!" Officer Kelly laughed. "Happened during a field trip. I just tweaked stuff to get out of latrine-cleaning duty."

"Nothing else, Monsieur?" I asked.

"Well," he said, "I did get everyone's Web browsers to show pages upside down."

I chuckled.

"What's so funny?" Monique asked, looking up from her kitchen work.

"You wouldn't understand, Monique," I said. "It's just a computer guys thing."

Back up in the wheelhouse, before the celebratory meal, we heard from Fred Montoya again. "Good news. I'm authorized to go as high as 500,000 euros. But that's it."

"Well, lamb meat first," I said. "Big thaw. Then we blow up the—"

"What are you talking about?" Monsieur Montoya demanded. "I've just added 350,000 euros to the original offer."

"Such a beautiful ship," I said in my most disappointed-sounding tone. "Surely it looks better in one piece."

18

THE PIRATES CELEBRATE

THE PIRATES' victory celebration happened near the bow area of *The Sea Mule* in a place empty of containers.

"Let us give thanks to our guns," Demon Killer said, and fired upward. "Praise God, praise us, praise the voice of the Almighty." The night rang with other shots. "Now let us join in prayer. Let us all thank our guns." Everyone fired yet again into the sky. "And now let us enjoy the bounty of our guns."

The feast began. Demon Killer, Monique, and the other pirates put their AK-47s down to dig into their lamb chops and Congolese-style rice.

Mpasi and I were up in the wheelhouse guarding the ship's key crewmen, so I didn't hear much except the AK-47 shots, but one of the celebrants later shared what happened.

Without any Purifier adults to get in the way in the wheelhouse, Officer Kelly meanwhile kept trying to reach out to us. "What puzzles me," he said, "is how a boy with your brains could be involved with Demon Killer."

"It's very complicated."

"How?" he asked. "You really want to spend the rest of your life on the lam from the law?"

"You don't understand," I said. "My parents..."

"Your parents what?"

"I don't help Demon Killer," I said, "they die."

"So he's extorting you," Officer Kelly said. "Nice guy."

"He killed his nephew. You think he wouldn't kill my parents?"

"What was that about?"

"Money. Splitting up the ransom."

"What makes you think he won't kill you?"

"I do my business with him, I'm done," I said.

"People like that, you're never done," said Officer Kelly, and turned to Mpasi. "And this means you, too. What about *your* parents?"

"Dead," Mpasi said.

"How?" Captain Chandler asked.

"Same people."

"All the more reason to stop them."

"They can make us rich," Mpasi said.

"Look at you," Officer Kelly said. "What a ratty uniform. You don't look rich to me."

"But how to attack?"

"You can untie us," Captain Chandler said, "and let us get our guns."

"But didn't you all surrender them?"

"Psst!" said the Captain. "There's a second cache."

"But didn't they bring their guns to the celebration?" I said of the Purifiers.

"They're easy pickings," Officer Kelly said. "Everyone together near the bow."

"Let me think about it." Mpasi said, and we both did. And acted. Officer Kelly's argument had hit home. If I kept going along with the Purifiers, what else would they have in store for me? And the same logic was working with Mpasi. So we went down to the ship's lockup and let the crewmen race out and from there into a secret gun room with hidden weapons.

THE CREW CAUGHT the celebrating pirates unawares as their festivities were winding down. A bullet in her oversized chest took down Monique. The crew killed most of the others. But Demon Killer himself managed to escape in a narrow path between giant cargo containers.

Crewmen herded the other surviving pirates into the lockup, while Captain Chandler got on the PA system to urge his men to keep looking for Demon Killer. All over the ship, men with flashlights prowled the halls. Captain Chandler told me: "You'll be picked up when we get to Boma. I can't promise what will happen next, but we'll put in our best word for you."

Suddenly, none other than Demon Killer showed up, brandishing an AK-47. "You looking for me?" he screamed. "Hands up, everyone!" And then to me: "And you—how could you betray the Général of all Générals?"

"What do you want?" Captain Chandler asked Demon Killer through me.

"A lifeboat to escape."

"Where to?"

"My gun will tell me." Then Demon Killer pointed to the detonator box on his belt. "You really think you can find all the bombs? A lifeboat for me, or I'll press the button and slay you all in God's name." And then to me again: "You've let me down. Don't you love your parents? I thought you were a good boy." Lost in his craziness, Demon Killer looked slightly heavenwards without foreseeing the possible consequence. "Praise God, praise guns!"

Then in a blink, I pulled out a pistol and shot Demon Killer in the forehead. I won't get graphic except to say he bled massively. Even in death, his bulk was overwhelming. It was as if I had toppled a statue rather than a putative human being.

Did I regret killing Demon Killer? Of course, for a second—no more, given all the people he'd murdered. Besides, if I myself wanted to live, I had no choice.

A relieved Officer Kelly rushed forward to congratulate me with a shoulder slap while Captain Chandler looked down at the Mighty Warrior's corpse and said, "Well, Lemba, no doubt about it—you *are* a good boy." Other crazies might yet imperil my village and my parents, but this one's soul was finally hell-bound.

Now I'll jump ahead and tell you what happened to Demon Killer and Monique's bodies.

He'd already killed Vangu, his own nephew, probably the only human who would have cared about Uncle Oscar's remains. Nor were any of the Purification Army faithful likely to step in. For Demon Killer had not been the most lovable of thugs, just the one handiest with an AK-47. I doubted that the Army would survive his death, now that fear of him could no longer glue it together.

Still, to forestall posthumous worship by any remaining Purifiers, an overcautious Kinshasa government burned up both Demon Killer and Monique and dumped the ashes into the Atlantic.

From what I'd learn later, the government didn't want his body left to revere. But if the avengers had known more about the man, they would have kept his flesh intact. Then

the Mighty Warrior himself could have become "fish food"
—the very fate he had so often wished upon his enemies.

IN MY NIGHTMARES I sometimes fantasize about a
Democratic Republic of the Congo under Demon Killer and
allies. Imagine all the people he'd killed on the way up. He
surely would have murdered even more once in power, if he
himself survived to cement his rule. I doubt he would have
lasted long, though. Luck and AK-47 skills and a network of
well-placed bagmen will protect you only so much.

But before the fatal bullets caught up with Demon Killer
in this alternative universe, he would have enjoyed
whooping it up with Monique in the domed Palais de
Marbre and the dozens of luxury SUVs and sports cars
bought with mineral and oil money. And oh—the possibilities for gun worship! No marriage or baptism would have
been lawful without at least a dozen shots fired in celebration. The Catholic Church would have survived, but only
underground, with countless priests fed to sharks and
brethren, and with myriads of young nuns sent to brothels. I
think back to the stories Demon Killer told of his degen-
erate father and of the rogue priest—imagine all the deprav-
ities and tragedies born out of this one man's sheer
warpedness. How merciful of the Almighty not to let
Demon Killer visit his misfortunes upon the entire DRC!

19

"KILL THE KILLERS"

PHIL KELLY, the communications officer, lunched with me in *The Sea Mule*'s mess hall and asked what I'd be doing with my life now that I'd put a bullet through Demon Killer's tattooed forehead.

I told him I wanted to return to Kinshasa and look for Josiane.

"No," he said. "I mean your future. Your work."

"I want to learn more about technology and earn my living in it."

"Don't get your hopes up, it's a long shot," Officer Kelly said, "but I know this computer science professor with a zillion friends and a good genius detector. Scholarship, anyone?"

"I'm only 15," I said.

"Well, let's give it a try. Dream! Go for it!"

Captain Chandler was at our table, and I asked, "What happens to me now?"

"I'm afraid that's for the local authorities to decide," he said.

"Will I see my family soon?"

"Just trust us, Lemba," Officer Kelly said. "We'll do our best for you."

FOR THE MOMENT, "BEST" turned out to be a UNICEF center for the rehabilitation of child soldiers. Mpasi went there, too, and both of us were patients of the center's therapist, Docteur Henri Dieza, a soft-featured man who favored ill-fitting jeans but spoke in a refined accent. All kinds of certificates hung on his walls. Did child-soldiers really care about the papers? I doubted it. Sympathy was another matter. Many must have valued it even from a stranger. Others simply must have hoped to talk their way out of the camp and go back to their villages ahead of time, with or without their parents alive to greet them.

"You two are both very lucky young men," Docteur Dieza told Mpasi and me. Mpasi listened with a calm expression that I'm confident matched my own. "Under current international law, you're too young to be tried as adults. So we'll instead prepare you to return to your families."

"My parents are dead," Mpasi said.

"Or train you in a useful trade," Docteur Dieza added. "All I ask is that you open up to me. Let the demons out."

Demons? The one still haunting us in our dreams, Demon Killer, was already dead.

"No demons," Mpasi said. "We were just boy soldiers trying to survive."

"Don't hold back," Docteur Dieza said. "We're smarter than you think."

Docteur Dieza turned his computer screen toward us—

it showed a picture of my tablet. "Exhibit A in your war crimes trial, Mpasi. It's all there. The hospital. The drones."

"I thought you said we were too young," I said.

"Actually, you are. No trial for either of you, and we'll do our best to keep this off the public record. A fresh start. Captain Chandler swears by you. I'm just making a point based on your computer files."

"*Merci*, Docteur," I said.

"Here's the plan. Therapy three times a week, one on one."

Walking out of the Quonset hut housing Docteur Dieza's office, Mpasi said, "I didn't know you kept a diary. That man knew everything."

"What diary?" I asked. "Must have been our emails to the support desk at DarkMarket. Or maybe—"

"Did you encrypt?" Mpasi asked.

"State of the art, available at the time."

"Whatever, they cracked it. Some hacker you are."

Mpasi and I played football that afternoon and returned to our bunk area to join some other boys watching a crime show. Two teenagers in the room spoke in what sounded like Kia-ese.

"Same old Lemba," Mpasi said when I noted the risks here. "Worry like a woman."

"They find out who we are," I said, "we're cooked. How'd you feel about people who bombed the hospital treating your wounded?"

What followed later that week, in Docteur Dieza's office, was a nightmare I *almost* wouldn't even have wished on Demon Killer.

I didn't see Mpasi reclining on a couch. But pressing my ear against the door, I could faintly hear his conversation with the Docteur when I arrived early for my own appointment.

"Do I have to?" Mpasi asked as the therapist went through a series of "and then whats?"

"You want the demons out," Docteur Dieza said, "you need to tell everything."

Mpasi was silent.

"OK, next time," the therapist said optimistically.

"And then," Mpasi went on, "I told them...where his parents lived...where they could kill them."

You can imagine the horror and anger I felt.

"There," said Docteur Dieza to Mpasi. "It is out...our secret. No one will ever know."

Later that day, Mpasi and I sat on a wooden picnic table silently eating with no others near us at the start.

"What's going on?" he asked. "You're so quiet."

"I'm thinking about what to do," I said. "About a dear friend who betrayed me."

"Betrayed you?"

"I didn't even suspect it," I said.

"So who is this friend?" Mpasi asked.

"I guess there's a little lesson here," I said. "You can be a victim and still be a bad person."

"Stop speaking in riddles," Mpasi said. "Just who?"

"Neighbors, almost. Know that bend of the river? We're right near the tip."

"What?" he asked.

"It's what I said to you. And you to Tiny."

"I don't remember."

"Don't remember? I'll give you something to remember." I bloodied Mpasi's nose. One more blow, and Mpasi fell to the ground. I had a good 30 kilograms on him. "You remember better now?"

"Well, maybe it happened and I forgot."

"Forgot? Am I that unimportant to you? Are my parents' lives that unimportant?"

I pounced on Mpasi and started choking him to the point where he was about to pass out.

Then I suddenly relaxed my grip. Mpasi took a swing at me, and the tussle started up again. The two of us rolled around on the ground, and later Mpasi got in his own blows. But I once again pinned him and resumed the chokehold.

"Exterminate all the brutes!" I yelled.

Then, yet again, I loosened the chokehold—I was back to my normal self.

"Am I a brute?" Mpasi asked.

We were so caught up in our fight that we didn't see a small band of Kias wandering around nearby.

"Maybe we both are," I said, "except I'm going to stop now."

I got up.

Mpasi wiped his still-bloody nose. "You almost killed me."

"We must not be our own brutes," I said.

"You're speaking riddles again," Mpasi said.

"You want a riddle, I'll give you a riddle. Why would anyone bomb a hospital?"

"It was Kia headquarters!" he screamed.

We heard some stirrings among the Kia spectators. But we were too angry at each other to care.

"It was a hospital, nothing more," I said. "A name sign, medics in white, children. How could it have been anything else?"

"It was a *Kia* hospital," Mpasi shouted.

"All life is sacred," I said.

"Demon Killer was right," Mpasi said. "'Kill the babies before they kill us.'"

The Kias moved closer.

"Murderers among us!" a Kia started yelling.

"Lemba and I," Mpasi said, "we're just playing a game."

"Kill the killers!" another Kia screamed.

The Kias piled up on Mpasi and me and started beating up both of us—pounding and kicking me into blackness.

20

UNIKEN DAYS: LET OTHERS BE EDISON

I WOKE up in a hospital with a nurse by my side. How I hurt, morphine injections notwithstanding! Later I'd discover that my face was badly bruised, my nose bloodied. Bandages hid the mayhem. The nurse told me I'd suffered a concussion. She asked if I knew my name, which I did.

"Where's Mpasi?" I asked the nurse.

"Your friend?" she asked.

"Well, sort of," I said.

"You were the lucky one," the nurse said.

"Me? All beat up?"

"Mpasi," she said softly, "is dead."

My life with Mpasi had had its ups and downs, but I still kept worrying about his soul. Would God send him to heaven even if he'd bombed the hospital? Mpasi had loved his parents and his baby brothers and, in all other ways, must have been a normal boy before Tiny and Sako turned him into a killer.

Of course, even if forced to murder their parents and hardened from there, many others would not have become eager hospital bombers. What had made Mpasi different? I'd hoped that in his place, I would not have gone on to commit evil, but who was I to know? Coaching Mpasi how to use drones, I'd been complicit to some extent in the hospital bombing. This was a far cry from dropping the explosives on St. Galois myself, and my efforts were hardly voluntary. Still, I'd been one step closer to being Mpasi. And in other drone raids I myself had bombed uninjured soldiers—alive and intact until my bombs fell.

In the sunroom of the hospital later that day, I took a call from my father, who, on hearing my voice, said, "Guess whose radio isn't working again. It wants you back to fix it."

"Any word on Josiane?" I asked.

"Our prayers go on," Papa said.

"I'll look for her!"

"When you're ready. Get better first! Just a minute. Bota wants to say hello to you." Bota, of course, was the first of the enforcers whom Demon Killer had sent to "guard" my parents and help out with farm work if I stayed in line.

"Thank you, Lemba, for killing Demon Killer," Bota said on picking up the phone. "You see, Demon Killer was threatening my parents, too."

Bota handed the phone back to my father, and I asked about Kodjo.

"He's fine," Papa said. "Treats Bota just like family. That's how we know he's good people."

Docteur Dieza and colleagues insisted on my spending several weeks in the hospital and the UNICEF center while they attended to my head and body. I myself was keen on rejoining my parents immediately. I'd suffered trauma every way, inside and out. But my parents would be the best therapists. Now I wanted to be at their side tending orange trees and otherwise losing myself in their daily routines. Then I would finally be ready to return to Kinshasa, look for Josiane, and perhaps work again at the Internet Café while preparing myself for bigger and better jobs.

But in the end I changed my mind. No, I would go *directly* to Kinsasha to resume the search. By now the odds were slimmer than ever that I would find Josiane, but I could not live with myself unless I gave it another serious try. Yet again I envisioned Josiane either dead or worn down to a physical and emotional husk. Oh, to rescue her before it was too late!

Then my thoughts wandered back to Internet Café; blessedly, Monsieur Zumbu wanted me back. "Such a wonderful man," Papa had said on the phone.

Even now I still found it hard to believe that the Purifiers were out of my life, and I wondered again if it would be safe to return to the Café after another few weeks of looking for Josiane. But then I remembered how Demon Killer had held together the Purifiers with fear, not genuine loyalty. Would he reincarnate himself to retaliate? And who else was left to care? No one, I hoped. But he still walked and talked and killed in my nightmares.

Monsieur Zumbu warmly hugged me at the Internet Café. "Come back! Please!"

The Café looked just as shabby as when Josiane and I had begged for jobs there. But something had changed. Pictures of both of us graced the wall, as if to suggest our presence had taken the place up a peg.

"I'll never forget your kindness," I said, "but Josiane's my real priority now." Back in Zane, people had even scrounged up a little money to finance my search. I was stretching it as far as I could, sleeping under overpasses while hoping that the cops this time wouldn't catch me.

"How I wish we could find Josiane!" Monsieur Zumbu said. "Oh, how everyone misses her!" He promised to give me plenty of time off to look for my sister. I didn't exactly say "yes" to him on the spot but came much closer than I dared expect. Just as before, I would have been able to live my life by the rhythms of rumba, both on and off the job. Can you think in music? I did. Again and again the sounds of Kanda Bongo Man would echo through my mind. "Amour Fou," "Malinga," "Lela Lela," "Sai Liza," "Kwassa Kwassa," "Isambe Monie," "Zing Zon," the others—I played them all in my head. Oh, and the great Franco, too, the musician-activist.

One day, strolling amid the clamor of Kinshasa in search of Josiane, I tapped the email icon of my Android cellphone and read a message from the University of Kinshasa: "The University is pleased to award you a full scholarship." I was to study computer science and engineering.

I jumped up and down, happily shaking my hands in the air—so wildly that I almost dropped the phone. "Oui! Oui! Oui!" You can imagine the looks I drew from puzzled onlookers.

"So this fall," I told Mama by cellphone, "I study computer science and engineering. Some Saturday nights maybe I can help out Monsieur Zumbu."

"But so young," she said.

"Well," I said, "you've got a young son with a very old brain. After university—a top programmer. Be nice to me and someday I buy you and Papa a whole room of TVs."

"And you'll still look for Josiane?"

"How could I not? I can look and study, too!" And I meant it. If my dreams came true, I could afford to relocate my parents to a safer place or at least pay Bota enough to stick around for a long time to guard them.

THE UNIVERSITY OF KINSHASA had enjoyed its moments, but in the mid-2020s now, amid all the fighting and chaos, it was hardly Harvard, Oxford, or the Sorbonne.

Some of the dorm rooms lacked either intact windows or mosquito netting, and unemployed graduates played Scrabble on nearby terrasses as a way to keep their brain cells alive. Around 30,000 students went to UNIKIN, the university's abbreviated name. Perhaps a Nobel Prize winner among them someday? I could only hope. If not immodest me, then maybe someone else?

I didn't know everything about the university in the beginning—remember, I'm Lemba writing years later—but I quickly learned. I got mosquito bites as part of my freshman orientation.

A white Catholic priest had helped to found the University decades ago as a branch of a Belgian religious institution during the colonial days. His bronze likeness, a bust, was in front of the Rectorat, the latticed administrative building with a stone façade at the entrance. Why? Of course, we owed the late Monseigneur Luc Gillon our thanks for his good side—for seeing us Congolese as more than farmers and fishermen.

But what to make of one of the man's priorities? He held a Ph.D. in nuclear physics, and within five years of the university's establishment, people there were bragging about their nuclear reactor. Just the ticket for upgrading my village's living standards, right? How different the Congo might have ended up with solar promoted from the start! As dedicated and well-intentioned as he seemed, even the brilliant Luc Gillon had been a captive of the technology and thinking of his time. I hoped I could do better.

Decades of neglect had happened in the wake of independence from Belgium—the science library at one point consisted of just a few hundred books. But I was set on making the best of my days at UNIKIN, and I loved the name of the Kinshasa suburb containing the university, "Lemba." That's right, the same as my first name.

I chided myself. Phil Kelly had meant only the best in getting me the scholarship, but even in my plight as a child soldier, maybe I should have held out for a better institution. So much of the technology I was taught at UNIKIN tended to be derivative. It was all well and good to be delving into tech at the Faculty of Science. But no small part of my coursework was just online learning from a Silicon Valley company that seemed mainly interested in training future technicians to fix its routers. A noble endeavor, I approved, but I already knew how to read a manual. I was just grateful I'd been spared most of the typical classes for new students.

As diplomatically as I could, I emailed Officer Kelly, who wrote back that my "real education" had yet to begin. I was confused. He replied that I would find out in time, after his main contact at the university had returned from a sabbatical.

Officer Kelly passed on some personal news. He said he would be leaving the Merchant Marine soon after hitting it lucky on an electric automobile stock. That would leave him with time on his hands when he wasn't working on a novel based on his sea-going, including, yes, his memories of the hijacking. When I told him of the less-than-Sorbonne level instruction that UNIKIN was giving me in literature, he asked if he could serve as my reading and writing tutor from afar. I of course jumped at the chance. Along the way, I learned a little more about Officer Kelly beyond his affinity toward me as another uppity techie. He'd lost his wife and three-year-old son in a plane crash, and now he saw in me the best of what his boy might have become.

Within a week, Officer Kelly express-mailed me a Kindle preloaded with literary classics, everything from Mark Twain to W. E. B. DuBois and leading African authors, and he started FaceTiming me to help me absorb the books. Twain had even written a pamphlet against King Leopold II, the murderous Belgian Demon Killer for whom millions of Congolese were demons.

Twain was white and dead, but I loved the way he showed up fools and liars, colonialists included. W. E. B. DuBois had died as Black as ever *in Ghana*. Was Officer Kelly, wittingly or unwittingly, telling me something? I wasn't quite ready to abandon my dream of life in America, but no longer so averse to living and dying in Africa. Oh to have been alive in the 1950s to whisper "Solar" into Monseigneur Gillon's ear and, even better, help bring the panels to every Zange in the Democratic Republic of the Congo and beyond! If I stayed, imagine what I could do with life-saving—not life-ending—drones!

Out of curiosity, I started tinkering with a design for a new way to propel drones faster and farther without a milli-watt more of battery power. But I lacked the cash to test my concepts fully and build a prototype. I emailed Officer Kelly for his advice and got back a response as cryptic as his note saying that my true education would come later. All he said was that "Providence will take care of you." Just one line—nothing more. Nor was he that informative when I followed up.

I needed a diversion to calm myself down amid the stress of looking for Josiane while going to school. With this in mind, I remembered my promise to Monsieur Zumbu. Yes, as a change of pace, I could work a few weekends at Pierre's Internet Café to help pay for the prototype of my possible invention. Dream on! That would still be a long way from covering the costs. Let others be Edison.

21

PAYBACK

I COULD TELL Monsieur Zumbu had been ballyhooing my return to his Internet Café.

Customers with familiar faces lined up outside to see my drone and DJ acts. Maybe they could even cadge some free Internet advice from me. I felt generous toward Monsieur Zumbu and the rest of the world and even wrote a scam letter for old time's sake, although I was outgrowing that.

With all the sweet rumba music, I easily fell back into my DJ routine. There was even a rumor that a famous bongo player might show up in the flesh. He didn't, but through our boombox he was very much with us electronically. So was Josiane, in a sense. I sometimes played recordings of her for appreciative customers and even listened to them in private. How I missed her! The Café would be familiar surroundings I'd shared with my dear sister. I promised myself I would keep scouring Kinshasa in search of her.

The next weekend, I made the bus trip again from UNIKIN, happy once more to see Monsieur Zumbu, flawed but familiar. In fact, I started making a habit out of it.

One Saturday after the last customer had left, I ran across Monsieur Zumbu inserting a bronze key into the door at the back to the café. He didn't notice me. Monsieur Zumbu opened up the door and a little boozily clopped down the stairs without bothering to lock the door behind him. Curious, I myself tip-toed down. Near the bottom of the stairs, girls shouted out to me from cages: "Please—help us!" I didn't have to guess: it was evident. I was in a subterranean brothel whose sex-slave occupants must have seen me as a possible savior.

Monsieur Zumbu took notice and spun around. "Upstairs, you snoop! Unless I kill you first." Once again I connected the dots. Had he imprisoned Josiane along with the other women in the basement to serve as sex slaves? Monsieur Zumbu's desperation gave me no choice but to believe the worst.

We scuffled near some stone stairs leading to a lower level of the dungeon. Monsieur Zumbu lost his balance and fell down them. I went for a closer look. Blood dribbled out an ear; he must have hit the floor hard enough to kill him. Given the horrors he'd very possibly had inflicted on my sister, I regretted he had died such a quick death. Normally I would never wish such suffering on others, but Josiane, after all, was my dear sister. I was not a brute. But I was a brother, and ideally, at least, Officer Kelly would have understood.

I reached into Monsieur Zumbu's pocket for his key set, walked back up the stairs, and went from cage to cage freeing his victims. Luckily, no customers were around at the time to object to his demise.

"My sister," I asked one of the sex slaves, "have you seen her? Josiane Adula." The slave pointed to the right.

"Keep walking," said another.

I did, and amid the happy shouts from the sex slaves,

ecstatic over Monsieur Zumbu's death, I kept yelling: "Josiane! Josiane! I'm here!"

No audible response. So I pressed on.

"Josiane! Please!"

And then came the return cry: "Lemba! Is it you?"

Josiane, clad in the leopard-spotted bikini that Monsieur Zumbu had wanted her to dance and sing in, was waving at me from behind an enclave with bars in front. Her looks gave no hint of her suffering. As noted, Monsieur Zumbu had been careful with his prize merchandise. But I could imagine the inner tumult coursing through Josiane's mind despite the resilience I'd known her for.

I unlocked Josiane. Crying out of joy, she embraced me. "Oh, Lemba, I thought you'd never find me. I missed you so much."

"And I was worried about you," I said. "If only I could have found you earlier!"

"It doesn't matter. You're here now!"

I tenderly wiped her tears, then unlocked the rest of the girls' doors amid their sounds of relief. Monsieur Zumbu's corpse could just lie there and rot. I'd rather free his victims.

Josiane was still weeping out of happiness.

"Now please stop crying," I said. "It's over now. Those dirty old men will just have to bid for someone else. I'll tell you one thing. I bet your favorite 'bidders' have missed you."

Hours later, Josiane's "favorite 'bidders,'" aka our parents, rushed forward to embrace us as we stepped off the bus in Zange.

Two days later, at least *looking* as unbreakable as ever, once again back to the normal world, my remarkable Josiane serenaded the crowd gathered to celebrate her return and munch on fried bananas and other treats. A big sign said, *"Nous saluons votre retour, chère Josiane."* I myself was now crying out of happiness. No telling where Josiane and I might end up in the world, separately or together, but our true home was where our parents were.

Reunited, I felt both proud of myself and disappointed, thinking I might have tried even harder to find Josiane. So much of the time she had been less than 100 feet from me in the basement of the café, yet she might as well have been 1,000 miles away, given my inability to find her sooner.

"Oh Lemba," she said, peeved, "you're too hard on yourself. You did your best."

I also wondered about a possibly bungled chance to locate her through Doka the Fixer. Regardless of the loathsomeness of both the man and his businesses, maybe I should have taken the database job at least temporarily. Perhaps Josiane would have shown up as part of Doka's ever-growing pimp empire, unknown even to him, considering the extent to which he was now farming out the sleaziness.

"My brother work for a pimp, even to find me?" she said before getting back to her singing. "Never!"

"But we worked for him before," I said while realizing that maybe I was too hard on myself.

"Before we fully knew what he was about," Josiane said. "Pimping isn't the same as pickpocketing."

Even more interestingly, suppose Doka had known her whereabouts but was keeping me ignorant until I'd fully justified his tentatively given trust.

"Maybe," Josiane said. "But who cares? I'm here."

Given all Josiane's time in the basement, I was just thankful she had held up better than I would have expected, both physically and mentally.

I was so caught up in my sister's rescue and the celebration that I didn't even think of something else—Monsieur

Zumbu's treatment of *me*. I'd taken it for granted that I'd just been kidnapped without his complicity. Now I remembered the bruises I'd seen on his face the day the Purifiers grabbed me. Had they beaten Monsieur Zumbu up to coax him into making me an easy kidnapping target in the stadium parking lot? Mpasi had betrayed me in regard to my personal safety—had Monsieur Zumbu done so, too? I *now* suspected as much. I could be a genius at devouring vast quantities of facts in a hurry. But like anybody else I could ignore the obvious when emotion won over logic.

Never mind that Monsieur Zumbu had been under pressure, and that I already knew of his cruelty toward Josiane. Reflecting on those bruises and our past friendship, I lost even more trust in my fellow human beings. Could anyone blame me? My weeping wasn't just over the miracle of Josiane's rescue.

22

LOVE AND WORK

I RETURNED the next day to the University of Kinshasa—only to find another reason for happiness, as well as a partial restoration of my faith in other homo sapiens.

Checking my cellphone in my dorm, I saw that someone had just opened a bank account for me, with a generous balance and a note saying it was for drone development. At last I could buy the best parts for a hardware prototype and customize further. In fact, I could even rent out offices for my endeavor. While aware of Phil's luck on Wall Street—yes, by now we were on first-name terms—I doubted he could have come up with the money solo. He kept mum for days, but then it spilled out. Whoever was to supply my "real education" had enlisted the aid of a secret benefactor.

Three months later, my first prototype was ready. No propellers anywhere—just rods sticking out of the fuselage. The drone made jerky motions as it cut through the air above an open field near the UNIKIN campus. But at least it flew. I put the video up on YouTube and bragged endlessly on social media. No way could anyone steal the idea. The magic was under the drone skin.

Was I still reckless in alerting the world within minutes of emailing Phil Kelly? Of course. I'm not perfect now in my 40s, and I certainly was not as a teenager. Needless to say, Phil did not react happily—just how could my mysterious backer trust me again? He said he'd have wanted me to keep my accomplishment secret until a formal public announcement.

As word spread, a French wire service reporter emailed me and asked how I'd grown so smart about drones. I said I'd just Googled and YouTubed around and checked forums on DarkMarket. I did my best to deny him clues. But through undisclosed contacts in the Kinsha military, he later glommed onto a troubling fact. I, Lemba, had been the master drone-operator of the Congolese Purification Army —the monsters who had bombed St. Galois Missionary Hospital.

"But Monsieur," I said, "I had nothing to do with it other than being with the Purifiers and training—"

"'Other than'? Does that really get you off the hook?"

"But I didn't do it. A boy named Mpasi—*he* dropped the bombs. Mpasi and others. *Horrible.*"

"How many more people did you kill?"

"Soldiers, yes—plenty. But you need to ask why I was in the Purifiers at all. They said they'd kill my parents if I didn't help them." I shared names and cellphone numbers of people who could corroborate my story. As luck would have it, Bota had stayed on with my parents as an enthusiastic helper.

The reporter grunted a few skeptical noises, then hung up, and I braced myself for a smear job.

So much for my drone dreams. Now no reputable businessperson would touch me. I would be a pariah. Even Phil might not speak to me again. So this is how I'd live out my life—as a mere gadget man, fixing old TVs and radios?

I dialed my parents to warn of the forthcoming story and make sure that Bota was handy by the cellphone just in case the reporter would give me a chance after all. But I couldn't get through—the line was busy. And when I did reach Mama and Papa, my fears only grew. Bota was off visiting friends in Kinshasa. What next? My expulsion from UNIKIN?

Just imagine my relief the next morning when I checked the wire service's Web site and saw not only an interview with Bota but a photo of him looking as fearsome as ever, a towering 200 centimeters. Based on a few hints from my parents, the reporter had caught up with Bota in person in Kinshasa. The wire service story bore the headline: "The Drone Whiz and the Machete Boy: How the Purifiers Made Them Commit War Crimes." The ultimate viral story! Scads of classmates offered their understanding and sympathy. Now I could be simply famous, not notorious.

All the fuss also brought me an email from a beautiful young artist enrolled at the university. Like the French journalist, she had tracked me down from the contact information I'd posted all over creation in my social media spree.

I liked Tyla Kudisa's elegant face and colorful but tasteful clothing in the photo that went out with all her emails. But her note was vague and simply told of an eagerness to discuss "our shared interest in peace." And her name was of Kia origin. I understood exactly why Kias had tried to beat me to death, and I lacked the slightest grudge against them. But I still was a bit wary and said I'd get back to Tyla later.

Besides, for the moment, I needed to focus on restoring myself to Phil's good graces.

I was in the middle of emailing Tyla Kudisa when a call came from the very man Phil said would provide my "real education." Kwame Ngoma in person turned out to be professor-formal, wearing a white shirt, tie, and dark, elegant suit. I wondered how he and Phil had befriended each other.

Then a man with shaggy blond hair and blue eyes joined us in the Professor's office. He wore tight-fitting black clothing and looked as if he would forever be above the sartorial concerns of mere mortals. I knew in a nanosecond who he was even before the Professor introduced us. "So here's the angel Phil was telling you about," Professor Ngoma said. "My old friend Jean Favre." The richest man in Switzerland and the rest of Europe!

How could I *not* have recognized Monsieur Favre? He was worth a good 450 billion euros, a fact seldom overlooked when the press wrote about him. Monsieur Favre had made his money in computers and telecommunications, and his philanthropic activities now encircled the ever-in-need planet.

"*Merci* for the funding," I told The Legend.

"Plenty more to come if you work for it," he said. "Lemba, do you know what social impact investing is?"

I in fact did, from all the Googling I'd done in my earlier quest for financial backing. "You invest to help humanity, not just make money."

"Well, Lemba," said Monsieur Favre, "I think your invention could do both. Imagine—a whole new propulsion system invented from scratch!"

"Monsieur Favre," said Professor Ngoma, "would like to develop you as a business partner."

"But why weren't you more open about it? *Both* of you."

"We were testing you," Monsieur Favre said. "Have you heard of cargo cults?"

I hadn't.

"That," he said, "is when some people think they'll get wealthy just because someone builds an airport. The cargo will fly in and they can just pray to the gods for their share. All over Africa, all over the Congo, there are fools like that—only, it isn't the imaginary airplanes flying in. It's the sleazy politicians promising the world to those who don't work for it."

"But we're not all that way," I protested, silently wondering if Monsieur Favre might be a little patronizing toward the masses who simply didn't know any better.

Monsieur Favre nodded his towhead. "Exactly, Lemba! We tested you, and you passed. No cargo cult! You've worked to get where you are, and you're still at just the start of your journey. Lemba, there's a new generation of Africans fed up with cargo cults. And you're one of the best. You'd rather learn and build than mooch and steal."

"So this is going to be my 'real education'?" I asked Professor Ngoma.

"Yes," he said, "and Monsieur Favre and I will do everything we can to help make your drone company happen. *Help make!* No cargo-culting. Without your sweat—nothing! And your brains, also."

I was still curious how Monsieur Favre and Professor Ngoma knew Phil.

"The Anatole France Society," Monsieur Favre said. "Docteur Ngoma, he's in there, too."

Thanks to Phil's tutoring, I knew who Anatole France was—a Nobel Prize-winning writer from the late nineteenth and early twentieth centuries. And most of all, I remembered the essence of one of his most famous lines: "The law, in its majestic equality, forbids the rich as well as the poor to sleep under bridges, to beg in the streets, and to steal bread." Yes, the fat cop in Kinshasa had been even worse. Imagine—expecting Josiane and me to bribe him for the right to spend the night under an overpass.

As it happened, the Anatole France Society was among the many Favre charities. If you couldn't afford international travel but had written a brilliant essay to read at the next annual meeting, the society would help you out. That was how Phil, just starting out as a seaman, had ended up at a Society event in Paris during a vacation period.

The Merchant Marine Academy's Humanities Department had once hired a literature professor in love with France's work, and Phil had responded. In time he especially liked Anatole France's novel *Penguin Island*. A half-blind priest in that book ran across an island of penguins and accidentally baptized them, turning the birds into human-like creatures, complete with a phony religion, crooked politicians, and terrorists. Demon Killer and his enemies in Kinshasa would have fit right in.

"You're a trained computer scientist," I said to Monsieur Favre on hearing of the Anatole France connection. "Why would you be in a literary society?"

Monsieur Favre laughed. "Oh, Lemba, you've hurt my feelings. Here I thought you might have read a few of my clippings. I can't tell you how many literature courses I took in college. What's the point of technology if you don't know how to use it wisely? Took lots of philosophy courses, too."

I remembered Phil's warning: "Whatever the technology, don't be a techno-brute—use it for the good. Don't be a brute of any kind." An appreciation of a humanist like Anatole France might help in that regard.

OF COURSE, this is mainly a war memoir, not a business one or full autobiography. But for the benefit of anybody impervious to mass culture, yes, my sister's Hollywood dreams became Hollywood reality. Same for Paris and London. Congolese rumba had gone mainstream the world over, and Josiane ended up the leading star.

I was as lucky in my own ways, and not just in school and business. You'll recall how I got into drones for the technology, but also to impress girls, like the ones by the swimming pool in that QuadKid ad. Well, indirectly, drones helped me find the love of my life—Tyla Kudisa. She was two years older than me, but who cared? I loved her soft, whispery voice, fine features, and well-kept, well-perfumed body, and she knew half a dozen languages. The art world was already taking notice of her sculptures displayed on the impeccably crafted Web page she had created on her own. More importantly, she cared about me and made it a point to learn my favorite recipes and my family history, which she then used to help win over my parents. Kodjo took an instant liking to her and the way she stroked his belly when he rolled over.

Tyla was actually just half-Kia—her father had married into a wealthy Bemba family in Kinshasa. But she was aware of the pain from the inter-tribal rivalries and reached out to me after learning of my sorrow over the massacre at the St. Galois Missionary Hospital. No, I hadn't bombed the hospital, but remember, I'd trained Mpasi and the other boys who committed the anti-Kia barbarities.

Just think—a country with hundreds of tribes, any one of which might be at war with neighbors or even just *friends* of neighbors. Together, my dear Tyla and I started a Web site devoted to the cause of inter-tribal reconciliation in line with "our shared interest in peace." I myself could be of Ngunda origins, if I extrapolate from old rumors about the orphanage and go by the demographics of Zange. Mpasi, alas, was from the same tribe. Tiny and Demon Killer were Kongos and despicable enough for their tribal leaders to condemn—after, of course, a helicopter crew dumped the Mighty Warrior's ashes into the Atlantic. Premature remorse could be hazardous to your health.

While I cared not the least about the high life, Tyla's luxury condo was a welcome change from the mosquito-ridden dormitory at the university. She was a gourmet chef and an accomplished hostess and helped me charm enormous piles of cash from Monsieur Favre and associates well ahead of time. The result was DA—Drones Afrique. Our main plant takes up more than 300,000 square meters in Kinshasa, and we are capitalized at many billions of euros. Imagine all the jobs created, even with robotic arms having sprouted up every which way in our factories. DA's training programs enroll former child soldiers ahead of others.

The first propeller-less drones from Drones Afrique were medical models able to fly drugs to the most remote villages and carry out blood samples and other specimens. Then came our large but extra-affordable drones designed to transport doctors and nurses for a fraction of the cost of competing models—and also evacuate patients to large cities for treatment. The upshot was millions of lives saved over the years in Africa and elsewhere.

And thanks to the same drone technology, we are now among the world's leading manufacturers of taxi drones, and we can give the Americans and the Chinese a run for their money. Many thousands of DA drones buzz above New York, London, Beijing, Paris, and Moscow, although it's a very quiet buzz, given our breakthroughs to lower the sound level.

The drones' batteries contain processed minerals from Congolese mines now free of child labor. Same for the self-driving electric automobiles that another division of Lemba Global, my parent corporation, exports. And speaking of batteries, we also reached out to miners to help them establish cooperatives to make batteries for e-scooters using local materials in part. My old friend Junior Boweya, proprietor of Brainy Scooters in Kinshasa, partnered up with Monsieur Favre and me on this particular nonprofit venture.

Monsieur Favre, at last just "Jean" to me, has not just achieved a social impact in the do-gooder sense. The Congolese people have helped increase his net worth—even though this was far, far from his main intent—while multiplying our own wealth. King Leopold II in reverse!

I HAVEN'T ANSWERED a major question. Just how we could have done so much in a violent country with greedy officials reaching out for bribes all along the way?

Here's how. Thanks to Drones Afrique and our sister corporations and related charities and advocacy efforts, the Democratic Republic of the Congo is more tranquil and far less corrupt. Our global image hasn't quite caught up yet with the truth—blame the usual racism, even now in the year 2050—but that will happen in time.

We discreetly reached out to brave student protestors at the University of Kinshasa, the nemeses of the tyrant in the overgrown presidential palace. Many of the brightest graduates became our employees.

Rather than just designing and manufacturing drones,

they and others helped us break into areas such as cheap solar energy and clean, sanitary wells, dug far more easily with the new technology we invented. Better disposal of solid waste likewise reduced disease. Our neighbor across the Congo River, the Republic of the Congo, formerly the French Congo, also benefited.

The fiber optic cables, cell towers, and satellite dishes we put in place made the DRC one of the best-connected countries in the world. Along the way, we helped start independent newspapers, websites, and broadcast stations that backed politicians with democratic tendencies. A dear cause of mine was the Buswe Institute, training future leaders in community organizing and democratic ways. We also helped pay for hundreds of schools with first-rate instruction in such heretofore neglected areas as civics, history, and even philosophy, so that people and technology could have more of a purpose. Massive grants and imported professors enabled the University of Kinshasa to expand and improve its teacher training. Politicians knew they would be watched in the future by smarter, better-informed citizens.

With some mines nationalized and the others fairly taxed, public revenue by far will be the main source of funds for life-changing initiatives, including better roads to help transport food. Taxes and ill-wrought regulations will be less of a burden on farmers hoping to invest in new equipment and engage in sustainable agriculture. Let the giant privately owned mining companies pay their share, just as Lemba Global does.

I'm also proud of our country's environment reforms. Logging companies can chop down many fewer trees in the Congo Basin thanks to our toughened laws and stepped-up enforcement efforts.

Under millions of our trees are bogs. Together, they

store a third of the planet's tropical peat, which helps soak up carbon dioxide. Short-sighted foreign greedsters thought they could exploit us and others and abuse the planet with impunity. Wrong. As shown by all the flooding in the UK and on the Continent, climate disruption is everywhere despite efforts like ours. Venice may vanish beneath the waves by 2100, and no telling what might happen to at least big patches of New York, Boston, Washington, Miami, Seattle, San Francisco, and Los Angeles.

Closer to home, the Atlantic has already claimed half of the seaside town from which Demon Killer launched his pirate raids.

The perfect Congo, of course, is still a long way off, environmentally and otherwise, even though we are no longer among the very worst hellholes on earth. Murderous militias still terrorize a few poor, isolated villages; and we have not been able to jail every crooked politician or bureaucrat in Kinshasa and elsewhere. But we are far better off than when I was a boy and Demon Killer-style monsters killed so many fathers, mothers, sons, and daughters in my nightmares and real life.

My allies and I didn't bribe anyone to accomplish our reforms and the rest—no Catch-22s here. But we did set up well-paying sinecures on the private side to distract the more dangerous and vain of the potential threats among politicians and bureaucrats.

Oh, how those sleazes loved unearned prestige and ceremony without substance! We even created a phony religion for Demon Killer types, with fake priests to assure them that guns were too godly to be fired with lethal results, except for the virtual kind in holy video games. None other than Tyla, benefiting from her family's countless contacts and her resultant knowledge, has helped shape our political and theological strategies. Sometimes she encourages my civic and charitable work by saying, "See, one man can make a difference." I tell her, "No. One man and his woman."

With our genuinely kind God smiling on us, how could Tyla and I have not smiled back by way of our own multi-billion-euro foundation making so much possible in areas such as health, education, and culture? Along with Jean, we founded a multi-donor national library endowment with a special focus on books and literacy.

How ironic! We in the Congo are becoming better read, while so many people in "developed" countries have let flickering screens steal away their capacity for sustained thoughts. Tyla and I love movies and video games, but they must never displace the written word. Books and libraries are among the ultimate enablers of prosperity and happiness. Same for education, another area where we set up an endowment. "Civilization," the novelist H. G. Wells once wrote, "is in a race between education and catastrophe." Exactly! And culture? It gives us a sense of humanity and the accompanying purpose.

We consider knowledge and culture to be so crucial that we do not expect the least profit in return for this charitable work. Of course, we still ensure that writers, publishers, and educators receive fair compensation.

Our writers and other intellectuals have spent years undoing the damage from "civilized" authors like Joseph Conrad. Few Africans outside the educated elites have read him, but his influence has survived in other forms. Conrad is one of countless reasons why Europeans felt free to keep stealing mineral wealth and so much else from us "brutes." Just how friendly to the Congolese people can a book be with expressions like "fool-nigger" used non-sarcastically? Yes, I know the subtleties. Conrad's apologists say he deplored the cruelty of the Leopold era, disliked Belgian-style imperialism, and at least tried to acknowledge our humanity. But never in *Heart of Darkness* does he depict us in detail as a people with families and dreams and music and art. That is the biggest turd in his dung heap. Are we not the same humans whose finely carved masks inspired Picasso?

The great Nigerian novelist Chinua Achebe once wrote, "All those men in Nazi Germany who lent their talent to the service of virulent racism whether in science, philosophy or the arts have generally and rightly been condemned for their perversions. The time is long overdue for taking a hard look at the work of creative artists who apply their talents, alas often considerable as in the case of Conrad, to set people against people." Today schools in the DRC teach Conrad to some students, but just as an illustration of how racism can befoul the brightest minds.

WHILE DOING our utmost to help uplift our country as a whole, Tyla and I have also taken care of the new generation of Adulas as well as my mother and father. Her parents were already more than comfortable. She and I were tempted to have six children, but to set an example for our birth-control campaign, we stopped at two. We've made up in quality what we lack in quantity.

George, 14, is already thinking of a career in artificial intelligence. He is coming up with a new way to use AI and nanotech to design and build skyscrapers at a fraction of existing costs. Over the summer, he will work as an engineer-designer in our self-driving car subsidiary and dabble on our solar energy side. No nuclear reactors are in sight for

George and other young Congolese. But our country has reached the point where we ourselves can export advanced technologies built on our genuine accomplishments, not imported foolishness like the old "Atoms for Peace" from the colonial days.

Nkama is two years older than George. A young ballerina, she is winning robotics competitions with elegant dancers indistinguishable from humans in looks, speech, and grace of movement. The idea isn't to replace people; rather, to see how far she can take the technology. She has inherited her feel for aesthetics from Tyla, who is still carrying off international prizes for her sculptures.

A future in robotics may well await Nkama. Then again, I might be a little presumptuous. My daughter's most salient trait is compassion, and she may instead train as a plastic surgeon to help serve the people disfigured by the mayhem of our earlier, less peaceful era.

Both Mama and Papa are alive, safe, and in good health—enjoying their 250-centimeter 3D TV, holographic marvels, pet robots, and a host of other techno-toys. A bit extravagant? Maybe. But the gadgets delight my parents, and cost is no obstacle. They still grow orange trees and cast their fishing nets in the river, but only because they enjoy remaining close to their neighbors in Zange. No longer must they struggle to eke out a living. The old rebuilt schoolhouse is gone. The principal at the new one was first in her class at the education school at the University of Kinshasa, and, of course, I could well afford to pay her to come to Zange.

Who would have thought that the Adula family would become so safe and so rich? But we are, in *every* way.

AUTHOR'S NOTE

Telling a fast-paced story, I have zeroed in on a small band of characters rather than fully plumbing all the complexities of the Democratic Republic of the Congo—both the joys and nightmares.

No, I have not done total justice to the nature of Congolese families, where grandparents, aunts, and uncles can play such prominent roles. I felt that my readers would care more about the characters—and about real Congolese —if fewer existed to keep track of. Uncles still show up, of course, including my major villain, "Demon Killer." To another character, he is simply "Uncle Oscar."

The ever-shifting political scene also does not get its full due in *Drone Child*. I've set the main story in a DRC of the near future, not today's Congo, so I do not have to squeeze in the dozens of factions of *real* rebels and others.

Also, keep in mind that most of the current conflicts are in the eastern part of the country (far from the fictional fighting in the Kinshasa region). President Félix Tshisekedi in August 2021 authorized American Special Forces advisors to go there despite the understandable trepidation of some

Congolese. News reports suggested they were to be in the Congo at least several weeks.

May the DRC not become an Afghanistan-style quagmire for the US! Congolese still bitterly associate the Central Intelligence Agency with the 1961 killing of Patrice Lumumba, the popular post-colonial prime minister. They also blame the US for letting Rwandan and Ugandan dictators meddle in national and tribal politics and militarily seize Congolese minerals. Of the millions dead in wars there since the 1990s, too many have died as a result of foreign intervention—African imperialism, abetted or tolerated by outsiders dishing out economic aid. Meanwhile, US firms from Costco to Visa and Starbucks have invested in Rwanda, which has backed murderous rebels in the Congo.

The rebel Congolese Purification Army is my invention with a little help from the late Ray Arco, a veteran Golden Globe judge who contributed to the movie script on which I based *Child*. A somewhat close real-life equivalent, the Lord's Resistance Army, metastasized out of Uganda to terrorize parts of the Congo. It has, yes, forced sons and daughters to kill their parents. Thousands of Congolese children have ended up over the years in either rebel or government armies. Citing the now-defunct Coalition to Stop the Use of Child Soldiers, the Council on Foreign Relations says some in the past have been made to kill relatives or even perform sexual or cannibalistic acts on enemies' corpses.

Horrors notwithstanding, certain poverty-driven children may even take their chances and become soldiers by choice. Threatening to halt some military training, the US has sharply reduced the Kinshasa government's recruitment of child soldiers. But governments and rebels elsewhere, not just Congolese militias, are still on the prowl for young AK-47 fodder.

Alas, so much of *Drone Child* reflects horrific realities. I invented the precise details of the gun worship of Demon Killer and the other Purifiers, but people somewhat like that do exist—if not in Africa, then elsewhere.

Hundreds of gun-lovers brought their AR-15s to rural Pennsylvania, for example, for a giant marriage ceremony in 2018 with the semiautomatics symbolizing "Biblical 'rods of iron,'" as reported in *Vice News*. I plead guilty if parts of this book seem like an allegory for politics in a gun-happy place like the United States. The number of people killed here is a fraction of those dying in Congolese wars, but gun deaths in 2021 were still the highest in decades—more than 47,000 homicides and suicides, according to the Centers for Disease Control and Prevention.

I also invented many locations, people, and two tribes. I did not want to risk being wrong about actual equivalents where they existed. The river near the home of my hero, Lemba Adula, is imaginary. It's not the Congo River, which shows up under its real name. The tall mountain range on the dramatic cover, the idea of the artist, would actually fit in more in the eastern Congo than the parts I write about the most. The Kia Tribe—Tiny and Demon Killer's foes—is fictional. So is the Ngunda Tribe, the possible tribe of Lemba and the definite one of Mpasi, his fellow child soldier. The name "Lemba"? Well, "Ko Lemba" in Lingala can mean "to soften, to exhaust, to calm"; certainly Lemba did his best to exhaust those who got in his way. "Mpasi" has many meanings in context but can mean "pain," as in childbirth or in other forms. It is most appropriate for the kind of life Mpasi ended up living and the cruelties he inflicted on others.

To be more precise, the majority of the Congolese names came from Junior Boweya. Although *Drone Child* is fiction, he and another fact checker-critiquer helped me ground my thinking in reality. I had relied on books, magazine and newspaper articles, online forums, YouTubes, and websites of groups like Human Rights Watch. But even as a novel, *Child* could never come across as authentic without guidance from Congolese people.

Junior is a translator, software localization advisor, and businessman in Kinshasa who dreams of starting an e-scooter business someday. With his permission, I wrote his hoped-for scooter business into *Child* to thank him. Yes, my endless appreciation, Junior! In case you're curious, Junior is Mungala (an Équateur-region tribe) by his father and Muluba (Kasaï region) by his mother. Junior vetted *Child* for accuracy and cultural sensitivity. He also gave me valuable editorial suggestions and other feedback from a Congolese perspective on the novel as a novel. Junior even passed on some rumors about real pirates living in the Congo, although we could not confirm that.

Press reports do tell of ship hijackings off West Africa. Any piracy by Congolese despite the tiny coastline?

Far more obvious, unfortunately, is the less than stellar DRC record of the United Nations, which Lemba briefly slams in Chapter 13. The Associated Press, BBC, and Africanews have told of some UN troops' crimes as well as their frequent fecklessness in preventing massacres. Infuriated protesters want the UN *out* of the eastern DRC and the government in far-off Kinshasa to do its job. Hundreds of armed groups are kidnapping children, killing, and raping in the Kivu region despite the presence of 20,000 UN soldiers and the expenditure of billions. Some rapist UN "peacekeepers" have also impregnated Congolese women, just as Lemba says. Thousands of blue-helmeted soldiers are well-behaved and dedicated, but the rogues' crimes have set back the efforts of all the troops. The US has been among UN troops' most generous financial supporters.

Let me add that Lemba's opinions on the UN, politics, and other matters are his own and not necessarily Junior's even though they are plausibly Congolese.

The same caveat would apply to my other fact checker-critiquer, Jean Félix Mwema Ngandu, a former Mandela Fellow and leader of a democracy-promoting organization called the Buswe Institute. I found Jean Félix through a journalist working for a well-known news organization. Junior I discovered through the Upwork agency.

Except on extremely minor details, the two fact checkers agreed. My applause to Junior for vetting that withstood vetting! Like Junior, Jean Félix hadn't any issues with cultural sensitivity—but oh how my fact-checkers saved my posterior on issues such as names and geography!

Something I did not invent is the loathsomeness of Joseph Conrad. By dehumanizing the "brutes" of the Congo in *Heart of Darkness*, he has at least unwittingly served as one of the many justifications for their exploitation. The Belgian childcare professor in Chapter Two is fictional, but other highly acclaimed intellectuals in different fields have joined Conrad in validating racist greed and cruelty. That would be the opinion of Lemba, my techno-genius hero, and I agree.

I got into Lemba's brain, by the way, partly through his techie side, having used and written about technology for decades. *Child* does not truly explore his Blackness or Africanness even though you cannot write about Africa and ignore race. Instead, this is far more a story of war, protective love of family, survival, and the moral conundrums of technology. I was pleased that Junior could identify with Lemba as a fellow tech-lover.

But how real is Lemba in the first place, with his multifaceted brilliance?

He is one of a kind and certainly *much* smarter than me; I haven't started any multi-billion-euro corporations lately. Countless young Africans are brainier than I am in their own ways. May they enjoy Lemba-sized success even if they aren't my character!

Now, on to the big question. Could genius not only invent new technologies but also help bring peace, prosperity, and honest government to a whole country? I admit the utopianism of it all even if there are and will be many Lembas or partial Lembas. But I can at least offer the scenario of, "What if things can go *right* in the Congo?" Maybe a few strands of my vision will help encourage young techies and political activists there and in other African countries. W. B. Yeats, the Irish poet, wrote that "In dreams begin responsibility," a line which inspired the title of Delmore Schwartz's most famous short story. So why not a variant? "In novels can begin realities?" Look at Jules Verne, having the gall in the nineteenth century to fantasize in detail of moon rockets.

But will the optimistic Lemba-style scenarios pan out? Hardly any guarantees! Think about all the wild cards such as global pandemics and the horrors of climate change, which could displace thousands and perhaps millions of Congolese—flooded or dried out and deprived of food supplies. But let me focus on some positives, such as the possibilities of changes in leadership.

Consider Jean Félix, for example. Born in Kinshasa 36 years ago, he belongs to the Baluba tribe (from the Haut-Lomami province, part of the former Katanga province). His father, a teacher's son who himself taught, served in a DRC parliament and held several other national positions. His mother, too, has been active in politics. Jean Félix has never held political office, as some have urged him to do. But he has done endlessly useful work within the nonprofit sector as the main founder of the Buswe Institute and Community Service Day, which, he says, in terms of the number of participants, is the largest volunteer effort in the DRC. His personal Facebook account has 3,000 followers and 5,000 Friends—just a fraction, obviously, of CSD's actual volunteer count.

No, Jean Félix has not turned the Congo into a tropical paradise; it remains mired in poverty and widespread corruption. But his efforts are a good example of the possibilities for change, ideally with plenty of encouragement from the United States, its allies, and elsewhere. Jean Félix's institute does not just serve as a think tank for progressive ideas for the Congo, it also trains future leaders in democratic ways and related areas ranging from community engagement to social justice. He himself was one of 14 Mandela Washington Fellows in 2015 from the DRC (500 for Africa as a whole). This is the flagship effort of the Young African Leaders Initiative, or YALI for short, that President Obama launched in 2010.

"Thanks to this program," Jean Félix told me, "I was able to go to Howard University, and I was also able to meet young leaders from other African countries who are bringing change in different ways in their own countries. This experience allowed me to build an important network in Africa and even in the USA. I don't know if there is still a single country in Africa where I don't know anyone. A lot of what I do today has been directly influenced by the program.

"Buswe Leadership Camp is a bit of a YALI in miniature. I hope it can grow even more like the Mandela Washington Fellowship. I hang out every day with amazing young people who won't all have the chance that I had to go to America to learn, but they are lucky to have me and others here to help them develop their skills. We receive a lot of testimonials from young people who have gone through this program, and we are proud of it."

No billionaires are behind the institute, though I'm 100 percent confident that Lemba would support it if he existed. "We had to do fundraising activities like selling t-shirts to fund our activities," Jean Félix said. "We have also received occasional support from individuals who find what we do important. But finances are a real headache. To participate in the Leadership camp, for example, young people pay a participation fee; this money allows us to cover the costs related to the camps. Not everyone is able to pay, so we often give spots to those who cannot afford but are really interested in learning. Young people with disabilities are often given free spots."

I asked how people could get in touch with Jean Félix to offer financial or other forms of help. His email addresses are busweinstitute@gmail.com and jeanfelixmwema@ gmail.com, and his phone number is +243812974329. He says the institute is officially registered within the DRC and has an active bank account.

What about Community Service Day? "The objective of Community Service Day is to bring Congolese in general, young people in particular, to contribute to the improvement of living conditions in their communities. The community service day was also created to spread the culture of volunteerism, service and self-giving in the Congolese community through actions of community interest." Volunteers "meet on the last Saturday of each month for various community actions; to support a noble cause, assist vulnerables—in short, respond to community problems on a voluntary basis." Thousands of young people, he said, participate in CSD activities in almost all the DRC's big cities.

So what inspired Jean Félix to create CSD? "I was a member of United Methodist Volunteers in Mission in Zimbabwe when I was a Masters student there, and also when I was in the USA, I had to participate in community service days. These different experiences as well as what I was already doing in the country allowed me to think about creating a structure that would allow the Congolese to participate" in activities for the common good. "Thanks to the CSD, we have been able to rehabilitate schools, pay for the education of hundreds of children, and much more."

I asked Jean Félix if he might run for a political office. "This is a question I get all the time now. In 2019, a rumor that presented me as the candidate for governor of the city of Kinshasa had gone viral. I had never seen such support, and I admit that I was even overcome with fear. At the same time, this episode made me realize that there are expectations and that a lot of people would see me in politics... The most important thing for me is to be able to contribute to change. Positions are not my priority. It's not about me but about building momentum with better political leaders for the future and truly politically engaged citizens..."

Two of the national issues for the politically engaged, beyond the terrorism in the eastern Congo, are the environment and election integrity.

Oil drilling and the like could help decimate rainforests and accelerate climate change, but with the war in Ukraine having jacked up energy prices, Kinshasa is keen on awarding new oil leases. Congolese officials say major powers haven't agreed to pay the poverty-stricken country enough to avoid this climate calamity. Time for Washington et al. to be more generous, as long as the spending of the money is sufficiently accounted for?

As for electoral integrity in the DRC, foes of President Tshisekedi have accused his supporters of election-meddling against opponents such as Martin Fayulu, a former Exxon-Mobil executive now a businessman and legislator. Claiming Covid concerns, police in September 2021 relied on tear gas to break up a *small* pro-Fayulu demonstration in Kinshasa, and along the way they beat a prominent journalist named Patient Ligodi after supposedly misidentifying him as a demonstrator. Later a government spokesman conceded that the police had used too much force to crush the protest. General Elections, including the presidential one, will happen December 2023. I'm updating this Author's Note months after the November 2022 Election in the United States, and I can't help but notice certain growing similarities between Congolese and American politics. So many US politicians have become tribalists for maximum self gain and job security at the expense of the common welfare and old institutions such as the electoral system.

Just as in America, the distribution of income and wealth is yet another sore spot, especially in regard to the Congo's gargantuan mineral resources. Consider—such a poor country so rich in cobalt, copper, good diamond, tin, and tantalum! In the region once known as Katanga province, reforms helped multiply local revenue from minerals. Congolese took over much of the production and refinement rather than simply exporting cobalt and copper, and the same also happened elsewhere in the DRC. Exactly as

Lemba would have preferred! Alas, not enough of the money ended up going for such purposes as schools, roads, health, and agriculture. But a law passed in 2018 is intended to change this and even make a percentage of mining revenue available to affected communities. May such be the case in reality!

In a somewhat related vein, President Tshisekedi has ordered the renegotiations of corrupt deals with foreign investors. Yes! Imagine the possible upside. Suppose enough wealth from minerals were available for a huge Norwegian-style sovereign wealth fund to help pay for everything from pensions to sustainable industrial investments domestically and abroad. Norway's Oil Fund is about $1.3 trillion or $240,000 per Norwegian. That's enough to help boost per capita GDP to some $90,000, one of the world's highest. True, the DRC has about 97 million people now, with more than 350 million expected by 2100—compared to Norway's current 5.5 million. But the Congo's raw mineral riches may total as much as $24 trillion.

Would each Congolese enjoy a Norwegian lifestyle after the government got its share of the wealth? From corporate tax rates to the amount of dividend revenue for the government, the planets would need to be sufficiently in alignment. Still, with stimulus from a gigantic wealth fund, dwarfing today's closest equivalent in the Congo, the per capita GDP could whiz past the present $580. And safer, better-paying jobs for miners could exist than the Dickensian ones in Siddharth Kara's much-needed exposé, *Cobalt Red*.

No, the money to develop resources all the way isn't available *now*. But the Congo could seek foreign investments from companies and individuals more reputable than the current variety in the mineral sectors. Start with a pitch to the socially minded Norwegian Oil Fund? Maybe foreign investment could grow with the understanding that the Congolese would sharply reduce oil drilling and other environmental horrors and spend mineral wealth transparently for the common good. The US used heaps of foreign cash during the nineteenth century to help pay for the new railroads and other infrastructure. Imagine the equivalent in the DRC. Money could go for industrial development, green energy and advanced telecommunications networks and drones and other means to help the country deal with its vastness and deliver goods and services more efficiently.

Let me add a warning, based on what Congolese themselves fear. Countless malefactors inside and outside the country *want* the Congo to be ungovernable and corrupt so they personally can steal more wealth, perhaps siphoning it abroad. Some members of the Congolese military are part of the corruption. Certain officials at all levels have a stake in it. Old tribal loyalties are another obstacle. Truly far-reaching reforms and other improvements could actually lead to more militia groups. Even so, given the rewards, such a risk is worth taking.

If the Congo thrived with the above scenario, it not only could ultimately reduce its economic dependence on boom-and-bust commodities but also forget the old Chinese model from decades ago. This would be in line with the vision of a brilliant Nigerian thinker, tech leader, and investor named Ndubuisi Ekekwe. Under his approach, the DRC would not end up just a source of cheap goods for the First World in a new era of robotics and artificial intelligence. Instead the Congolese could become robust consumers of their own goods. Also, they could trade more with other African countries while using AI to scale up local innovations. Not an impossible dream in the land of rumba.

Talk about local creativity applied to areas such as product design, aesthetics included!

Combine that with expanded and much-improved education so Congolese people can in fact master the technology at all levels and in time make their own contributions to it. Let enough of the mineral money pay for the education and training. In *Child*, one of Lemba's children is using AI in his engineering work, and a daughter is considering a career in robotics as one possibility. Go Adulas! You're far richer than the average Congolese, but with fairly shared resources, many more will enjoy opportunities.

Returning to this book's backstory, I'll also thank my editor, Dave Pasquantonio, for his incisive critiques and production help. Props, too, to my talented cover designer, Nate Allison of Hidden Gems Books, who picked up elements of a vision from the super-gifted Eli Bavar at BavarArt.com.

My appreciation likewise to my early readers, especially Marta Steele of Editing Unlimited, Bob Snyder of Channel Media Europe, Liz Hock, Robert Nagle of Personville Press, Mack Truslow, and Melinda Jackson-Jefferys. Also thanks to Susan Chaires, my lawyer, and Jewel Hart, a book marketing expert. Jewel and Eli, along with my friend Karen Heilman, helped me come up with a new title after I discovered that the world was not falling in love with an earlier one, *No Taller than My Gun*. The replacement title better conveys the nature of the book to people not already familiar with it.

As is already clear, *Child* started out as a movie script. I wrote at least 90 percent of it, but the script includes such gems from Ray Arco as Mpasi's fish-hawking at sea, and I also benefited from Ray's general feedback on it regardless of our constant disagreements. He was the one who asked, "Wouldn't Demon Killer wear some kind of ring?" Of course —hence, my vision of AK-47- and RPG-emblazoned variants! Ray was a Romanian-born Jew who had survived Demon Killers with swastikas before making it to Hollywood, where he was a film importer, symposia coordinator, concert tour manager, education activist, and Romanian-language newspaper columnist, while trying his hand at 3,000 poems, 51 books, and 36 film-scripts, lovingly edited and archived by his wife, Ileana, a self-made museum curator. Nothing happened, alas, except a little volume of poetry in the U.S. and some now-forgotten minor film collaborations abroad.

I'm not surprised. Ray could promote others but all too often floundered at marketing projects that might enable him to move out of the crowded West Hollywood apartment where he'd lived for decades. He pushed the *Gun* script as a children's story just right for 12-year-olds, regardless of the body count. An old-fashioned Hollywood eccentric-optimist!

Only in photographs did I see Ray's beret and goofy clothes below—we never met face to face. Instead, as editor-publisher of a Virginia-based ebook site, I got this phone call out of the blue ordering me to delete a comment that included his private phone number. No telling why the number had gotten there, but I obliged since the entry strayed far from the cosmic issues of the day such as Kindles vs. iPhones for ebook junkies. As optimistic as ever, Ray asked if I might be working on a novel or script. Imagine—a Golden Globe judge soliciting material from *me*.

Child began, as *No Taller than My Gun*, after Ray said George Clooney might want a child soldier script because of his wife's prominence as a human rights lawyer. The *Gun* title came to me almost immediately. It was my variant of a quote from an ex-child soldier in Burma, now known as Myanmar: "My gun was as tall as me." That became the title of a report from Human Rights Watch, to which I added my own metaphorical twist, letting the giant Demon Killer say: "No man is taller than his gun."

Did either Clooney actually read the script? Who knows? But meanwhile Ray could dream, and I could write and rewrite while pondering, "Will he gracefully recuse himself when we're up for a possible Globe?" Yes, Ray did just a fraction of the scriptwriting. But he was really into *formatting*. The industry standard for script margins and the rest wouldn't do—we had to stand out. One day he said somebody at Netflix wanted to check out our project. But then Ray and I spent weeks going back and forth over the script's exact appearance, and the opportunity passed. What better way to avoid rejection and keep dreaming—just don't show your work in such situations? More positively, Ray prodded me into writing this book. Thanks, Friend! I'm sorry you weren't around to finish reading it and then pester me over the margin width.

To answer the inevitable question about a 60-year Golden Globe judge born in 1929, Ray at times could be a man of his era on racial issues. He wanted the script to depict some Congolese women as "exotic."

"Please no," I said. "To the other characters they're *local*." Wives and daughters and sisters and cousins and lovers and friends, not tourist attractions!

But wait. This same man from the start loved the idea of drawing a Black director into the project, and he took a keen interest in anti-poverty, educational, and environmental issues affecting minorities, even writing a master's thesis on such topics. He worked with indigenous peoples in Canada and also met with the late Senator Robert F. Kennedy to see about forming a nonprofit youth organization.

Ray fell while shopping, slipped into a coma, and died of Covid in the hospital on Christmas Day 2020. I'd begged him to write a will for his family and prepare a list of his contacts to help me follow through on marketing the script if he were no longer around. Ray balked; he absolutely knew he'd make it to 100. His beloved Ileana died two years later.

I'm just sorry I couldn't say good-bye. I'm delighted to have been, as described by Ray and Ileana, "the American in the family."

—David H. Rothman, Alexandria, Virginia—updated February 17, 2023

Addendum: Dec. 1, 2025: Drone technology has advanced since the writing of this book. Just the same, the basics hold true. In *Drone Child*, Lemba uses his mastery of drones to outwit far more powerful forces, and Ukranians are doing the same in their fight against the Russians. No need to tell which side I'm rooting for!

But what about political developments in the DRC and related ones in the Unitesd States? So many have happened that I won't be able to keep up with them in my author's note. But I'll soon be updating the blog at dronechild.com.

A DISCUSSION GUIDE

FOR BOOK CLUBS, SCHOOLS, AND LIBRARIES

In *Drone Child,* a genius child soldier struggles to survive and to save his family from machete-wielding terrorists. He later rescues countless other people.

Below are 34 discussion questions about *Child* for book clubs, schools, and libraries. You need not answer all of them, just those most appropriate for you or your organization.

Why not pick out the 10 best questions for your own use?

#1: What are the ways in which Lemba Adula, the brilliant protagonist, "rescues" others besides his family? I'm using the R word both literally and figuratively.

#2: Mpasi, Lemba's fellow child soldier, ends up eagerly committing atrocities. Why has he succumbed to indoctrination from the Congolese Purification Army, and why has Lemba resisted it? How much do Mpsai's war crimes stem from the trauma of being forced to kill his own parents and baby brothers? To what extent do other explanations count for both boys, such as upbringing and innate qualities?

#3: Lemba is peaceful by nature but loves technology. How does he reconcile this enthusiasm with the reality that bad people can use drones, computers, and other tech for evil purposes?

#4: The Purifiers give Lemba a choice. He can either become a military drone whiz and help slaughter hundreds of people for these barbarians or see his parents shot or macheted to death. Which option would you choose and why?

#5: Can the case be made that the Purifiers aren't genuine soldiers but rather gangsters in uniform? Instead of fighting a genuine civil war, might they instead be engaged in a series of criminal actions? To what extent do they really believe in their cause, as opposed to a chance to plunder, rape, and kill?

#6: Lemba's parents were both orphans. What's the significance of that, in various respects?

#7: How do his parents pave the way for him and his sister to succeed in life? Why have they taken such constructive interest in their children? Not all parents would to the same extent.

#8: People in Lemba's village care about education. How much has this *community* interest also contributed to the success of Lemba and his sister? Why do parents in some places value education while others don't?

#9: How did Josiane, Lemba's sister, help him get ahead (and vice versa)?

#10: What do you like and dislike most about Lemba as a person? How do you feel about Josiane?

#11: In what ways could Lemba and Josiane serve as role

models for teenagers and other young people in violence-plagued communities in the United States or elsewhere?

#12: How reliable a narrator is Lemba? Are there any places in the book where you distrust him? Is Lemba *always* credible?

#13: What do you think of Lemba's decision to remain in the Congo rather than depart for America or another country with many more educational and professional opportunities?

#14: Why does Lemba marry a woman from a wealthy, influential family? Are love and shared values the only reasons? Is there any opportunism here, either financial or otherwise?

#15: Monsieur Favre, a fictional Swiss philanthropist, is helpful both to Lemba and the Democratic Republic of the Congo. But in the real world in Africa, would a First World philanthropist care as much and have such pure motives? Why or why not?

#16: To what extent might the Democratic Republic of the Congo be a more peaceful and prosperous country today if European colonialists had not murdered and exploited millions of Congolese?

#17: Many of the ancestors of Black Americans came from the places now known as Democratic Republic of the Congo and the Republic of the Congo. Does America owe the current inhabitants any reparations? Should Europeans whose countries colonized the Congo also make amends?

#18: How could trade and foreign aid policies be more helpful both to America and poor countries like the Congo? Please note that the Democratic Republic of the Congo is a major global source of strategic minerals used in electronics and other industries.

#19: Long term, would the DRC really benefit from

establishing itself as a source of low-cost goods for First World countries? Or will robotics and artificial intelligence make this model obsolete? How could countries like the DRC adapt?

#20: Ecologically, the Congo is important for its tropical rainforests, which, if destroyed or thinned, would mean more disruptive climate change. How could corrupt politicians there threaten the country's ecosystem and the world's?

#21: The Democratic Republic of the Congo is among the world's poorest countries. How and to what extent is corruption responsible? Are there any lessons here for First World countries like the US?

#22: Virtually all the people hating each other in *Drone Child* are Africans. But intertribal wars can be as fierce as those between people of different origins. How is *Child* an allegory of US race relations and politics (among other battlegrounds)? Would the same idea apply to parts of Europe, with tensions over its own ethnic and religious differences?

#23: Just what politicians outside the Congo does Demon Killer, the Purification Army leader, remind you of? In what ways?

#24: What events in Demon Killer's life most contributed to his monstrous sadism?

#25: How are the gun worshippers in the novel comparable to those in the US? "Gun worshippers" in this case means people who literally worship guns, as opposed to, say, gung-ho collectors or target shooters.

#26: Countless novelists have depicted Africa as a dark continent without also spotlighting such positives as artistic achievement and the idealism of certain political leaders there. Has such fiction set back social and economic progress by reinforcing stereotypes? Did Joseph Conrad, author of the classic novel *Heart of Darkness*, do more than his share of damage? Should books like his be banned from school or instead be presented in context as reflecting the racism of their times?

#27: Is all the violence in *Drone Child* necessary, or is it unavoidable because this is a war novel? Would omitting the most disturbing violence from books like *Child* even be a disservice to society? Might it at least somewhat reduce the possibility that people would fully understanding the damage war does, including the civil variety?

Prepared in consultation with Karen L. Heilman, M.Ed. Vetted by Jean Félix Mwema Ngandu and Junior Boweya.

No, the above questions do not cover everything. Here are more questions from Junior himself:

#28: Back when Lemba was just a school kid in his village, he repaired TVs and other appliances. How easy do you think it was for Lemba to familiarize himself with electronics?

#29: What could have been the mental tools used by Josiane to deal with the horrors she experienced in Monsieur Zumbu's basement? How might she have coped afterwards with the traumas without showing her inner scars?

#30: Are local people solely liable for the violence and chaos in the Democratic Republic of the Congo, or might some external influences from other countries be involved?

#31: What possible strategies could government officials in Africa use to end interethnic conflicts in rural areas such as the ones depicted in *Drone Child*?

#32: In the globalization era, what can African emigrants do to address situations like those described in the book—how can they help?

#33: After reading *Drone Child* and learning the story of this African boy, would you like to visit the Congo? If yes, would it be for tourism or something else? What else if that applies?

#34: What impact has the story made on you now that you've finished the book?

LINKS IN AUTHOR'S NOTE
AND DISCUSSION GUIDE

Author's Note:

—*The Atlantic*'s mention of soldiers eating the hacked-off arm of a torture victim and threatening to eat her husband's heart:

https://www.theatlantic.com/international/archive/2012/04/a-congo-mother-survives-cannibalism-to-save-her-children-why-her-photo-matters/256405/

—Examples of fighting in the Democratic Republic of the Congo in recent years:

https://en.wikipedia.org/wiki/Kivu_conflict

—Background on President Félix Tshisekedi: https://en.wikipedia.org/wiki/F%C3%A9lix_Tshisekedi

—VOA report on President Tshisekedi's authorization of the deployment of US special forces in the eastern part of the DRC:

https://www.voanews.com/a/africa_dr-congo-accepts-us-military-help-against-adf-militia/6209612.html

—A blog item by one of my fact-checkers, Junior Boweya, reflecting the concern of some Congolese that the

Congo might become another Afghanistan if US military presence grows:

https://www.dronechild.com/blog/d27xca3rnxryv8xm buam8esf7xskon

—Patrice Lumumba, the first duly elected post-colonial prime minister:

https://en.wikipedia.org/wiki/Patrice_Lumumba

—On US-Rwandan ties, including investments:

https://theconversation.com/the-us-and-rwanda-how-the-relationship-has-evolved-since-the-1994-genocide-188115

—A Hollywood Foreign Press Association biography of Ray Arco, the late Golden Globe judge who contributed to the film version of this book:

https://www.goldenglobes.com/articles/remembering-ray-arco-hfpa-member-1929-2020

—Background on the Lord's Resistance Army, one of the models for the Congolese Purification Army. It has in fact forced children to kill their parents:

https://www.chicagoreviewpress.com/first-kill-your-family-products-9781613748091.php

—A chilling example of gun worship in the United States:

https://www.vice.com/en/article/4avkdw/rod-of-iron-ministries-purchases-property-in-tennessee

—*Vice News*'s article on a wedding ceremony with semi-automatics symbolizing "Biblical 'rods of iron'":

https://www.vice.com/en_us/article/zmw5e5/pennsylvania-couples-celebrated-their-nuptials-by-bringing-ar-15s-to-the-church

—Wikipedia item on Lingala:

https://en.wikipedia.org/wiki/Lingala

—The Facebook page of the invaluable Junior Boweya, a fact-checker for *Child*:

https://www.facebook.com/boweya.junior

—News accounts documenting the UN's less than stellar record in the DRC:

https://apnews.com/article/abbc13a929264889a110d2bb2c ccfo1f

https://www.bbc.com/news/world-africa-38372614

https://fr.africanews.com/2018/10/09/rdc-des-images-qui-pourraient-embarrasser-la-monusco/

—On the Kivu region, the setting for so many military conflicts over the years:

https://en.wikipedia.org/wiki/Kivu

—A French-language Website from Jean Félix Mwema, the former Mandela Fellow who was my other fact-checker:

https://jeanfelixmwema.wordpress.com/

—About the Mandela Washington Fellowship:

https://www.mandelawashingtonfellowship.org/leader ship-institutes/

—Facebook page for Jean Félix's Buswe Institute:

https://www.facebook.com/busweinstitute/

—Upwork agency, through which I found Junior:

http://www.upwork.com

—On the Baluba tribe, to which Jean Félix belongs:

https://en.wikipedia.org/wiki/Luba_people

—On the Haut-Lomami province, home of the tribe:

https://en.wikipedia.org/wiki/Luba_people

—It is part of the former Katanga province:

https://en.wikipedia.org/wiki/Katanga_Province

—Facebook page for the Busy Institute:

https://www.facebook.com/busweinstitute

—About Community Service Day, which Jean Félix says in the largest volunteer effort in the DRC in terms of the number of participants:

https://www.facebook.com/csdvolunteers

—Jean Félix's personal Facebook page, with 3,000 followers and 5,000 Friends:

https://www.facebook.com/people/Jean-Felix-Mwema-Ngandu/100008465467980

—United Methodist Volunteers in Mission, an inspiration for Community Service Day:

http://umcmission.org/united-methodist-volunteers-in-mission-2

—Links related to environmental issues:

https://www.cfr.org/article/democratic-republic-congo-drc-auction-rain-forest-oil-gas

https://www.washingtonpost.com/national-security/2022/08/10/congo-rain-forest-fossil-fuel/

https://www.washingtonpost.com/business/energy/to-save-the-planet-poor-nations-need-to-get-paid/2022/07/27/073ee736-0e09-11ed-88e8-c58dc3dbaee2_story.html

—Tribalism explained:

https://www.theatlantic.com/magazine/archive/2018/10/the-threat-of-tribalism/568342/

—Reuters report on the beating of a journalist and tear gassing of demonstrators during an election-related protest:

https://www.reuters.com/world/africa/police-beat-journalist-fire-tear-gas-during-congo-election-protest-2021-09-15/

—About Martin Fayulu, a major political foe of President Tshisekedi:

https://en.wikipedia.org/wiki/Martin_Fayulu

—South China Morning Post report on President Tshisekedi's order to renegotiate a $US6 billion copper and cobalt deal with a Chinese consortium:

https://www.scmp.com/news/china/diplomacy/article/3151840/chinas-african-resource-infrastructure-deals-face-growing

—On the risks of the DRC simply being a source of inexpensive goods for the First World—written by Nigerian thinker and entrepreneur Ndubuisi Ekekwe for the *Harvard Business Review*:

https://hbr.org/2019/09/why-africas-industrialization-wont-look-like-chinas

—Background on Ekekwe:

https://en.wikipedia.org/wiki/Ndubuisi_Ekekwe

—*Africa's Sankofa Innovation*, a book by Ekekwe, about an ancient African system promoting innovation:

https://www.amazon.com/Africas-Sankofa-Innovation-Ndubuisi-Ekekwe/dp/1980419701

—Statistics from *The World Population Review* on the DRC, whose population might double from the current 90 million by 2047:

https://worldpopulationreview.com/countries/dr-congo-population

Even allowing for factors such as increased use of birth control, the increase should be vast.

—Web site of my editor, Dave Pasquantonio:

https://www.davepasquantonio.com

—Nate Allison, the cover designer.

https://hiddengemsbooks.com

—Eli Bavar, the artist, parts of whose vision Nate picked up:

http://www.bavarart.com

—Marta Steele of Editing Unlimited, an early reader of *Child:*

https://www.editingunltd.com/

—Bob Snyder of Channel Media Europe, another invaluable source of feedback:

https://www.channelfocuscommunity.net/sample-sites/

search-by/state?value=Channel%20Media%20Europe%
20Ltd

—Robert Nagle of Personville Press, still another:

http://www.imaginaryplanet.net/weblogs/idiotprogram
mer/

https://www.personvillepress.com/

—Jewel Hart, a book marketing expert, who, along with others helped me come up with an optimal title for *Child*:

https://chicklitcafe.com/about-us/

—"My Gun was as Tall as Me," a report from Human Rights Watch on child soldiers:

https://www.hrw.org/reports/2002/burma/
Burma0902.pdf

—*BusinessInsider Africa* on the 25 poorest countries in the world. The DRC is the fifth poorest, with a GDP per capita of only $457:

https://africa.businessinsider.com/local/markets/
mapped-the-25-poorest-countries-in-the-world/f2tg0wr

Note: The ebook version contains some links I had to drop here for space reasons.

Discussion Guide:

—Political commentator and novelist Lucian K. Truscott IV on how "a 21st Century American Civil War" could turn our cities into bloody battlegrounds and roil everyday life—not just kill countless people:

https://luciantruscott.substack.com/p/what-would-a-
21st-century-american?r=f6qk&utm_campaign=post&
utm_medium=email&utm_source&fbclid=IwAR0Sm-DwNS
bJSr_-R_8XqGOGI-YJBtoNFgor3tTWEVrwOJI-
Gxpghcd2SWE

Truscott was not saying a civil war would definitely happen—rather, telling what it would be like *if* it did.

ABOUT THE AUTHOR

David H. Rothman is also the author of a Washington novel, *The Solomon Scandals*, which *The Washington City Paper* praised for "the same dark zeal Hammett held for Frisco or Chandler had for Los Angeles."

A former poverty beat reporter, Rothman has long been interested in the technological side of international development and the topic of human rights. His family lost distant relatives during the Nazi era in Germany, and he is a judge in a major journalism competition on rights abuses, which, to this day, continue in the Democratic Republic of the Congo and countless other countries, including the United States.

But how does a pale-skinned white novelist in Alexandria, Virginia, get inside the head of a genius child soldier in the Congo? Through Lemba's tech side, partly, along with plenty of online and offline research.

Rothman had help from another technology fan, Junior Boweya in Kinshasa, a translator, software localization expert, and businessman who fact-checked *Drone Child* and otherwise offered an invaluable Congolese perspective. So did Jean Félix Mwema Ngandu, a former Mandela Fellow and prominent civic leader. For more information, go to DroneChild.com. You can reach Rothman directly at davidrothman@pobox.com.

www.ingramcontent.com/pod-product-compliance
Lightning Source LLC
Chambersburg PA
CBHW021333190726
48288CB00003B/1085